plastic fantastic

plastic fantastic

Simon Cheshire

DELACORTE PRESS

Published by
Delacorte Press
an imprint of
Random House Children's Books
a division of Random House, Inc.
New York

Text copyright © 2004 by Simon Cheshire
Cover photograph copyright © 2006 by Tara Moore/Getty Images

First published in Great Britain in 2004 by Piccadilly Press Ltd.

Visit us on the Web! www.randomhouse.com/teens
Educators and librarians, for a variety of teaching tools, visit us at
www.randomhouse.com/teachers

Library of Congress Cataloging-in-Publication Data
Cheshire, Simon.
Palstic fantastic / Simon Cheshire.
p. cm.
Originally published: Great Britain : Piccadilly Press, 2004.
Summary: When fifteen-year-old Dominic, pop music fan, and Lisa
Voyd, singer and icon with the band Plastic, are stuck together in
an elevator, the encounter results in drastic changes of attitude
for both of them.
ISBN 0-385-90243-3 (glb.) — ISBN 0-385-73213-9 (pbk.)
[1. Bands (Music)—Fiction. 2. Popular music—Fiction.
3. Fans (Persons)—Fiction. 4. Interpersonal relations—Fiction.
5. England—Fiction.] I. Title.
PZ7.C425213Pl 2005
[Fic]—dc22   2005041264

The text of this book is set in 10-point GillSans Light.

Printed in the United States of America

March 2006

10 9 8 7 6 5 4 3 2 1

BVG

**To all us fans,
and the world of fandom**

"There's 32 reasons why I love you
All but four of them are true"

—"32 Reasons," from the Plastic album *From Hell It Came*
(Voyd/Parkins © Cellophane Music Ltd)

12:27 p.m. This is the greatest moment of my life.

I am stuck in a lift with Lisa Voyd.

Me! I, Dominic "Sherlock" Smith, aged fifteen and eight months, of 21 Victoria Crescent, have felt the lift shudder to a halt, have seen the lights on the panel of buttons flicker and go out, and now I am stuck inside with . . .

Lisa! Voyd! THE Lisa Voyd: lyricist, style goddess, lead singer of Plastic. She's standing barely half a meter from me. I think my heart is about to burst with joy! I think my head is about to explode with sheer delight! I think I'm about to hyperventilate!

Calm down, Dominic. Breathe sensibly. Come on, come on, be objective, be rational.

This is a once-in-a-lifetime opportunity. This is what you've always wanted, Dom, me old mate. This is THE moment. It will never come again. It will be over in two minutes, as soon as the lift starts moving again, as soon as they get the power back on. Make the most of it, be cool, and above all make a good impression on her.

"Hallphreeelllblee," I burble. Oh crap, my mouth's stopped working.

She turns and looks at me. Looks at me, properly, for the first time.

"You OK?" she says.

I don't want to burble again. So I nod instead.

"Are you . . . freaked out by lifts or something?"

I shake my head, noooo, no no no, no problem.

Her eyes narrow slightly. Her face now has the exact same expression as in the photograph of her in the May issue of *MusicMaker*, page seventy-four, top left-hand corner. That exact mix of the quizzical and the exotic. She is the page come to life.

It makes her look even lovelier than usual. She is slightly taller than me, almost six feet, and the chunky-heeled boots she's wearing make her even taller. She seems slimmer in real life, her figure hugged in dark-shaded clothes which couldn't look more expensive if they had *This cost a fortune* stamped all over them. Black jeans, flappy at the ankle; a thin, military-styled jacket over a regular shirt; a tie, around her neck instead of her collar.

She reaches out once again to stab all the way up the column of lift buttons in turn. Her fingers are long, with neatly clipped nails. They're slightly ragged at the lower edges, though. I think maybe she picks at them.

Her neck is slender, her jawline sharp, her nose a bit more flared than it registers on camera. Her face is broad, kind of angular, and her eyes are the darkest I have ever seen. Science fiction eyes. The hair that's the envy of so many girls is indeed a shining tone of reddish auburn, cut in a straight, short chop-chop style that highlights the exquisite beauty it surrounds. She is six months past her twentieth birthday.

I'm close enough to catch the scent of her shampoo. Even her smell is beauty incarnate.

This person is gorgeous, talented, self-assured, powerful, respected. Everything you could aspire to. Everything I could look for in a woman. Utterly wonderful.

And I am here with her, in this lift that is stuck. For a moment, my eyes shift focus to the glass wall beside her and I see my reflection. There stands Dominic Smith, whose tinted specs make him look dead cool, thank you very much, although the scraggy black hair manages to spoil the effect. My hair stages more uprisings than a nineteenth-century revolutionary. I inherited it from my dad. Thanks, Dad.

But that IS me, reflected in that glass. Tallish, thinnish, borderline gangling. Standing next to her. I can see both of us at once. Both of us, her and me, me and her.

Me and Lisa.

There's movement outside the glass. It suddenly reminds me of what's going on outside. There are feet jostling about just above the level of our heads, and below us a ten-meter drop to the shop floor of Big Deal Records.

You see, the lift has glass walls, and glass doors so you can see the mechanism inside that opens and closes them. Very interesting, actually, I've never seen that before. Only the floor and ceiling aren't see-through. They were lit up from behind when the power was still on, a bright, clean light that danced around Lisa's boots in neatly irregular shapes.

The lift is stuck halfway between floors, halfway between the cavernous space below that is the main atrium of *"Birmingham's Latest, Greatest Entertainment Retailer"* and its second floor (*"More Fabulous Bargains Upstairs! Chart Albums—Two For £20"*). A thick band of concrete blocks our view in a strip around three sides of the top half of the lift. Above the band, we can see shoes dashing about in the small gap which is all that's visible of the second floor. Now and again, half a face appears, squashed to the floor, on its side, one eye staring in at us. OhmyGod! Lisa Voyd's in there with some kid! Who's the kid? Does anyone know who this kid is?

And from lift floor to waist level, we get a panoramic view of the crowd below. Hundreds, packed into the shop for its grand opening. *"Lisa Voyd Here in Person! Saturday at Noon! Signing Copies of the New Plastic Album."* Shouts and wild looks and the occasional scream get thrown up at us now that they all realize something's wrong. OhmyGod, she's stuck! The lift is stuck! But wait, who's that devilishly handsome young man with her? Can he save her? Will he hug her tightly to allay her fears as terror and claustrophobia take hold of her?

"Holy CRAP!" Lisa is stabbing at the buttons once more. Nothing responds.

"Don't panic," I say, with fantastic calmness and authority.

Her head whips around and she glares at me. "Who the hell is panicking?" she says calmly. "Do you see me panic? Is this panic? No. I'm just sick to death of this bloody lift!" She gives the button panel a sharp smack with both palms.

I don't think it's her slapping which makes the lift lurch, but at that moment it definitely lurches. The lights in the panels above and below us flash and blink. Both of us stand absolutely still. My eyes go like saucers. A loud, yelling scream rises up from the crowd. The lights die again.

"Hey, it's just like *Thunderbirds*," I say, before I know what I'm saying. She gives me a look that could melt rock.

I nearly drop the armful of signed CDs I'm carrying. It occurs to me that Lisa still thinks I'm one of the shop's back-room guys. She doesn't know who she's brought in here with her.

I kneel and pile the CDs up in the corner. The clattering of their cases seems horribly loud in this confined space. Lisa's face gazes up from each and every one of them. The floor of the lift is waxy, brand new, unmarked by the trudging of bargain-hungry shoppers.

I sit with my back pressed into the opposite corner. With an exaggerated sigh, Lisa sits too. She flashes a dismissive glance at me and pulls a phone from her jacket pocket. It's red and silver, not one of the newer models. Its edges are scuffed; I'd say it had been tossed around quite a bit, probably kept in a bag with a load of keys and stuff.

Correct me if I'm wrong here, but I don't seem to have made that good impression I was so keen on, do I? Come on, come on, it'll be too late if you're not careful. This thing will get moving in a minute. Tell her your name, at least! Tell her something she'll remember.

Lisa keys in a speed-dial with her thumb.

"My name's Dominic."

She hits the little telephone symbol. The phone disappears beneath her auburn hair.

"My name's Dominic."

"You said," she says, without looking up. "I know your name, you know mine. Makes me feel warm and fuzzy."

Whoa. She must be feeling really nervous. The Lisa Voyd I know and love is never rude to fans.

For a second or two it's strangely quiet. The burbling of the crowd is muffled by the glass, and the scuffling of shoes above seems to have slowed down to a mere frenzy.

"Bob?" she says, keeping her eyes down. That'll be Bob Fullbright, Plastic's manager. (Her parents have a dog called Bobby, but I don't think she'd be phoning the dog at a time like this.) "Bob? Yeh! Yeh!" Her face is hidden by her hair, but I can tell she's smiling; there's a smile pasted onto her voice. "Yes, but when exactly? We've got to be there by two, haven't we? Yes, I know, but . . . Well, hurry them up! For Christ's sake . . . I am not panicking! This is not panic! This is anger! . . . Yeeeess, yeeees . . . What?"

She holds the phone out to me. "He wants to talk to you." Obediently, I take it. It's warm from her hand.

"Hello?"

Bob Fullbright's voice is a tinny screech. Phone distortion makes it sound even worse. "Who the HELL are you? What are you doing in there?"

"Umm, being stuck?" I crane my neck and peek through the glass to see if I can spot him on the shop floor, but he's out of sight.

"You DARE try anything and I'll have you broken into pieces!"

"What? No, I—" Then Lisa snatches the phone back and begins to argue with him, but I'm not listening because I'm wondering why he didn't phone her first. You'd think that'd be the first thing he'd do. And he'd surely assume that it was me who'd stopped the lift. But apparently not.

Lisa switches the phone off and tosses it across the floor. It clatter-bounces hard; if it could speak it would be saying "aarrgrgh."

She sits silently for a moment. She puffs her cheeks a couple of times and seems to have resigned herself to the situation. Then she shuffles over to me on bum and heels. "Do you mind if I sit there?"

I vacate my corner immediately. "Sure."

"My manager says I should stay as far out of sight as possible. Give the photographers less to aim at. Apparently the papers are down there already. The TV crews will arrive any minute. I have to keep my phone off too. Reporters will be ringing me nonstop now. Jeeeezus, today of all days."

I sit across from her, with my back to the glass. It shields her from a sizeable chunk of the shop floor below.

"Thanks," she says quietly. She looks at me, holds me with her dark eyes. Suddenly I find I can't meet her gaze and I give an embarrassed snort.

"I gather we can't get moving yet?" I say.

"This building is so new, this lift so high-tech, so brilliantly designed, so computer-controlled, so secure, and so safe, that the shop manager's got to get specialist engineers in. They've been called, so Bob says."

Specialist engineers.

Which means a little more time with Lisa Voyd. Not two minutes after all.

"Thank God I had a pee before I got here," she says.

Given a little more time, I think even I can make a good impression. Yup, this is the greatest day of my life.

"I have a small confession to make," I say. She looks slightly alarmed. "Actually, I'm not on the staff here. I'm just a fan. I'm your biggest fan. Plastic are my whole life."

She shuts her eyes gently and lets out a long, long, long, slow breath. "Great," she whispers. "I've mistaken a fanboy for a shop assistant. My idea of heaven. OK, fanboy, how are we going to pass the time?"

A few ideas flash through my head. None of them are very practical. I'm not sure I like being called fanboy. Surely it's . . . no, no, I remind myself, it's not actual rudeness, it's just nerves. This is Lisa Voyd, remember.

I've got my iPod in my coat pocket, but as most of what's on it are Plastic tracks I doubt she'd be interested. She's said in loads of interviews that she rarely listens to her own work.

"I have a pen," I venture at last. "Have you got any paper?"

"Nope. Write on the glass."

"It's a ballpoint."

End of conversation.

I look down, through the glass. I can see Tim and Tanya! They're almost directly below, their faces straining upward, their expressions exploding with happiness and jealousy. Tanya shoots out a thumbs-up. Tim is calling something but I can't hear a word of it. I send them a tiny little wave.

They're surrounded by other fans and bewildered security people, who are one size too big for their suits, and the yellow T-shirts of Big Deal Records' shop assistants. I glance down at my own T-shirt beneath the open zip of my coat. Slightly different yellow, but you can see how someone might mistake me for staff.

There's a fan in a bright green pullover, pointing a video camera up at us. There's the store manager, a balding man with an ID badge, yelling at the crowd and biting his fingernails. There's a knot of ten-year-old-looking girls wearing Plastic sweatshirts, flipping cheerfully through the CD racks.

"Wow," I breathe. "They're all here for you."

"So they think," says Lisa quietly. "Why are you a fan, then?"

I find I have to look at my shoes. I can't tell her just how much she means to me. "Because Plastic are the best band in history. Because you're the greatest songwriter in the world. Because of who you are and what you do." That's all I can say. It's not one atom of one scrap of the steadfast mountain that is my allegiance to all that is Plastic. But that's all I can say. My shoes don't seem very impressed.

Lisa sighs. "There were plenty of bands I liked before I started making records," she says, "plenty who inspired me, some I adored." She points through the glass. "But . . . this, I don't understand." She looks back at me. "How can a throwaway pop band like Plastic be your whole life? What kind of wasted life are you leading?"

It is 12:38 p.m.

"You and I deserve each other
You're fantastic, I'm a stunna
One hundred percent of lurve"

—"100% Love," from the Plastic album *From Hell It Came*

(Voyd/Parkins © Cellophane Music Ltd)

The precise moment my life gains meaning, by turning into Plastic, is on the way to Blenheim Palace. At least, theoretically we're on our way to Blenheim Palace. In actual fact, we're on our way to really cheesing off a stream of drivers on a busy road in central Oxford. Which is quite a long way from Blenheim Palace.

"Yes, I know, I know," says Dad, his teeth more gritted than a motorway in a sharp frost. You can tell he's on the point of detonation because he's leaning forward over the steering wheel so that he's almost lifting himself off the driver's seat. He does that when he's close to the point of detonation.

"I don't know if you realize," says Grandad slowly and carefully from the back, "but we've been on the road over two hours now."

"Yes, Grandad, I realize that," says Dad. I'm guessing about thirty seconds to meltdown.

"Oh. Aye. Well, I was just wondering if you'd realized, like."

Granny squidges round in her seat. "Did you need to stop, Sidney love?"

Grandad considers it for a moment, like the brave little soldier he is. "No," he says, slowly and carefully, "I'll be all right."

Mum's sitting in the front, up next to Dad, desperate to have her say. You can tell she's desperate to have her say because she's so still and quiet. It always follows the same pattern: it gets to the point when Mum can't contain herself any longer, then she says something blindingly obvious à la Grandad (like father, like daughter), then that sets Dad off, then there's a huge argument, then there's complete silence until we get wherever we're going. In this case, we're going the wrong way up a one-way street.

"Dammit, dammit, dammit, yes, sorry. SORRY!"

"I think we should have turned left at the last roundabout," says Mum. Which is blindingly obvious.

"Oh SHUT UP!" shouts Dad. "I KNOW that. I KNOW! I'm not STUPID!"

There you are, see? I was right.

"If you knew, then why didn't you do it?" says Mum. Her voice has now got that spitting cobra twang to it, in which her original Lancashire accent starts leaking out of her words and she starts stretching vowels all over the place.

"I know NOW," says Dad. "Of course I know NOW! . . . Yes, SORRY! SORRY!"

Another driver coming the other way makes a series of gestures which Mum and Dad don't realize I know the full meaning of.

"SORRY!"

The trouble is, you see, that Dad never uses a map. He refuses to. He says that his damn taxes have paid for all the damn road signs disfiguring the country and he's damn well going to use them and he'll be damned if he's going to fork out again for maps when there are damn great sheets of metal stuck up every hundred yards telling you where things are. You'd think he'd have learned by now. You'd have thought ALL of us would have learned by now that even uttering the phrase "day out" is enough to start tempers coming apart at the edges.

Once Mum and Dad are well into the swing of things, my little brother, Sebastian, gets going. He's seven years younger than me. He is a creepy, miniature version of me, and is currently going through his evil-little-brat phase.

"Muuum, I feel sick."

"Christ, that's all we need," growls Dad.

"Dad! Don't be like that! He can't help it!" barks Mum.

Seb's perfectly fine, of course. It's his evil-little-brat phase talking. I can even see his evil-little-brat grin in the car's wing mirror.

The only thing that appears to be preventing a major accident at the moment is the size of the car. It's a people carrier, an ugly great Fiat Multipla which looks like a mechanical frog from the front. It's tall enough for the oncoming traffic to spot it and veer out of the way with an almighty screech of tires. Mum and Dad only bought the thing so that all six of us could fit in it when we go for a "day out."

"Pull over here! Here's a lay-by!"

"I do have eyes, Mum, I can actually see the lay-by, thank you," says Dad.

The radio is on low in the background. When Dad drives it's normally Radio 4 or BBC7. It's not that he doesn't like music, it's just that he can't stand DJs. They really rub him up the wrong way, for some reason. When Mum drives it's always whatever thumpy-thump local station she happens to find first. Today, however, Mum seems to have won the Battle of the Station Presets despite being only the copilot.

I think it's fate. I think it's meant to be. Because it's at this moment, right here, when Dad is pulling away at the steering wheel and illegally parking in a disabled space, when Mum is holding her tongue and Seb's hand, when Gran is clearly off in a world of her own and Grandad is rubbing his knee and considering a few new medical conditions he could try out. This is the moment that the wonderment of Plastic enters my life for the very first time.

An irritating mid-Atlantic voice on the radio says something I don't listen to. (Come to think of it, I hate DJs too, how genetically horrible is THAT?)

And then it marches through the speakers in the car doors. "100% Love," first single, already huge in the airplay lists. Of course, I don't know that yet. I wasn't listening to the DJ, was I?

How have I missed this before? Where did this come from?

PA-DOWWWW! PA-DOWWWW! Ba-ba-ba-ba-ba-ba-ba-ba!

It makes me smile. Why haven't I heard this before?

And then . . . she starts to sing. And my heart dissolves like sugar in a hot cup of coffee. Her voice is as clear as glass, as dark as night, as hard as nails, as soft as something really small and fluffy.

Utterly beautiful.

I've always loved pop music. I've always loved its insistent presence and its so-what attitude. But I've always loved it in small pieces—a chorus, a turn of phrase, a particular song, or the way somebody looks. And suddenly, now, it's the complete works.

It's like I've waited to hear this sound all my life, as if I never knew there was something missing in my ears until this moment. I lean forward in my seat. I've got to hear it better. What did that DJ say it was called? Who is this? Who are they? Who's this singing? What a FANTASTIC piece of music!

"Dominic, you're not going to be sick too, are you?" says Dad.

"No, Dad, I'm trying to listen to—"

"I'm OK now," says Seb, grinning. "I'm hungry."

"You'll have to wait till we get there," says Dad.

"You can have a sandwich out of the cool box," says Mum. "Dad, can you reach the cool box, by your seat?"

"Can we all be quiet a minute?" I say. "I'm trying to—"

"No, I can't reach the damn cool box, he'll just have to wait till we get there," Dad said.

"Well, Dad, we're not getting there very quickly, are we?" says Mum. "We do still have to eat."

I've got to hear the end of this song! I've got to hear who this is!

"Ooo, look at the lovely roses they've got in that shop," says Gran.

"Granny, they're plastic!" says Seb.

"They're noooot," says Gran.

"They are!" says Seb. "Can't you see the sticky label on them?"

"Please!" I say, loud enough to shut people up, but not loud enough to start them moaning at me. "Can I just hear—?"

"Ooo," says Gran, "that's not fair, is it? Pretending plastic roses are real. I'll go and box their ears for them, I will! Ooo, I'm a right terror, I am!" And then she emits one of her immense giggles, and that's that. Nothing can penetrate the wall of sound that flies up when my grandmother starts laughing. I can't even hear the traffic.

So I miss the mid-Atlantic voice again, and then they're on to some dreadful rubbish from the 1990s. I'm . . . well, let's just say I'm slightly peeved, just a bit, just a tad. No, Mum, I don't want a sandwich!

But that music is in my head now. I roll it round and round my mind, and it still sounds incredible.

I'm not paying any attention to the journey anymore. I've got something far more interesting to pass the time: thinking about who that might have been, and when I might hear it again.

By the way, we do, in fact, in the end, get to Blenheim Palace. It is completely boring.

Then, when we get home, I turn on the radio in my room. I flick channels, up and down the wavebands like a pacing tiger. I get snatches of this and that and the other, nothing terribly exciting, nothing like THAT SONG.

I go to bed feeling vaguely disappointed. It niggles me when I can't get to the bottom of something. I take my radio into the bathroom the next morning, tune it to the same station as was on in the car and prop it under the pedestal that holds up the sink. I endure a stream of pointless babbling (jeez, I really don't like DJs, do I?), and I listen to one chart-busting smash hit after another, but there's not a single note of the one I'm after, and not a single mention of any band I've never heard before.

At school, I hum the thing to Emma and Tanya and half a dozen others. Blank looks all round. Whatever it is, this song, this band, this sound, I think to myself that I must be in on the ground floor. I must have spotted something that hasn't entered the mainstream yet. I've recognized talent that's above and beyond the norm, and I've got to it first. It makes me feel rather smug about my discerning taste in music, but gets me no nearer to finding out what I want to know.

But then, as I said, "100% Love" is actually getting a vast amount of radio airplay at this time. All day, I assume that I'm looking for the proverbial needle in a haystack, when all I've been is slightly unlucky not to have tuned in to it already.

I get home, zip over to the radio in the kitchen, and then as I head for the fridge . . . THERE IT IS! For the first couple of notes of the intro, I don't recognize it. I can't have caught that bit in the car. But then I let out a short yelp and stand still, one hand on the open fridge door, the other raised for silence when there's only me in the room, as if I need to shut myself up. As if I need to shut the whole world up, just for a second, so I can listen.

It makes me smile all over again. The bumping technobeat, pure mainstream pop, tweaked with highs and lows which jump out and surprise you as if they were poking fun at the whole idea. An infectious, rolling guitar tune that's picked up here and there with synthesized trumpets and violins, a big, self-conscious music that's unlike anything else. Verses which make you want to dance, a bursting chorus which makes you want to dance faster. This is the template for the whole Plastic sound.

And that voice . . . HER voice . . . Wow, if she looks as good as she sounds, I think my eyes will melt. Shhh! Shhh! It's ending! Prattling DJ!

". . . Plastic, and '100% Love.' Fantastic band, that's their first single, out next Monday, it's ten to five, news coming up at five, but before then more new singles from . . ."

Next Monday.

What day is it today? Tuesday. Oh, nuts.

Even so, I feel a sense of quiet triumph. I've hunted my info-prey through the broadcasting jungle and now I've moved in for the kill. "100% Love." By Plastic. What a brilliant name for a pop group.

I make myself a cheese sandwich, somehow sensing that things are different now. I've turned a corner, I've crossed a river, I've . . . whatever geographical metaphor you want to use. There's no going back. Life has changed for the better. Life has turned just a little bit Plastic.

In the living room, I pick my way through the TV guide in the nest of stuff beside Grandad's armchair. Let's see, pop programs, pop programs . . . no mention of Plastic appearing on anything. But then this only goes up to Friday. If the single is out on Monday, they'll surely be shoved in front of cameras all weekend.

I can't believe how keen I am to get a look at them! Someone at school had been saying the other week—Emma, presumably, it's the sort of thing she'd say—that pop music is all pop and no music. Any old rubbish sells if it looks sparkly enough. And I agreed with her. And yet, here I am, flicking through the music magazines in the newsagent's to try and get a look at them!

And why not? I've found out who they are, and now I want to find out what they look like. Well, what SHE looks like, anyway, a-hem. And what her name is, of course. But it's the sound they make that attracted me, isn't it? That's the important point. I'm not being bowled over by image, or marketing, or any of that doodoo. It's the music that counts. Nobody can question my artistic integrity, thanks very much.

Of course, if Plastic turn out to be a bunch of chinless student types in pullovers I'm going to be hugely disappointed. Yeah, OK, I'm shallow. But I'm not going to make myself look like a dork, now am I? I mean, am I?

But I need not worry. I should have more faith. I get my first look at Plastic on Saturday morning, on one of the kids' channels.

The program blurb in the (new issue) TV guide only includes the words "featuring Plastic," which isn't exactly helpful. I sit through over two hours of Japanese cartoons and assorted other stuff which quite frankly would bore anyone with an IQ that reached double figures. Seb comes wandering in and sits glued to it, though. Which proves my point, really. But anyway, either I'm a naive mug or TV presenters must do a course called Effective Audience Lying Techniques: when they're jumping about at the start, telling the world what wonders are going to be on today, they say that Plastic "will be with us all morning, they'll be performing their new single for us very soon." Wooo! Yeah! The rent-a-crowd of kids in the background wave about like multicolored seaweed.

There's obviously a whole new definition of the term "very soon" being used here, because Plastic get two and half minutes while the end titles are running. Is that any way to treat the new gods of popular music? I don't think so.

But I'm not all that bothered really. Not now, because I've seen them. I've watched them play that music. I've gawped at the screen, afraid to blink in case I miss something, while the names of producers and makeup people and camera operators slide by underneath.

There are four of them: three guys who look like they're in their early twenties, and the female singer, who I'd guess is a couple of years younger. The drummer has an aggressive splat of blond hair which looks as if it'd squeal like a piggy if you ran a comb through it. He's got a look on his face that isn't saying anything polite, and he's whapping at a bank of drums like they were snapping at his hands and he was having to keep them in control. There's a keyboard player with glasses, who doesn't look up once from his leaping fingers. There's a bass guitarist, with his guitar slung around his chest at an unfashionable height and a moon face that would make a baby look tough and grizzled. He clearly can't believe his luck that he's on national telly, even if it's only as a runner-up to the Japanese cartoons.

And then there's the singer. She grips her microphone stand and hauls it around with her just to make it clear that she don't take no nonsense from electronic sound equipment. She belts out the lyrics with unashamed passion, and she gazes directly into the camera whenever she knows it's gazing directly at her. She doesn't dance, or anything like that—she's not that kind of pop star, they're not that kind of band. She just kind of pulses to the beat, like she was living it.

Two and a half minutes. And then they're gone.

Wow. I think my eyes have melted.

Monday, Monday, Monday. No weekend ever seemed so damn long. Actually, it's a whole new experience for me, wanting a weekend to be over and Monday morning to come a-knocking with its sickly grin and its time-to-go-to-school-again deodorant.

Of course, the shops are still shut on the way to school. Before I get into class, I weigh up two alternatives: (1) keeping zipped about Plastic's performance and just waiting for the rest of the world to catch up with me, or (2) asking people whether they saw Plastic's performance and thereby admitting I spent Saturday morning in front of the Japanese cartoons.

As it turns out, Tanya brings up the subject first. Did I catch that new band on TV? They were really good, weren't they? What were they called again? She is not in the slightest bit embarrassed about watching the Japanese cartoons in her jim-jams and pink bunny slippers.

Emma gives us both a boggle-eyed stare and does the old flattened-hand-zipping-over-the-head bit. She was at her Saturday job in Birmingham. No, she didn't see the repeat on Sunday, she was practicing for her piano lesson. Ooh, *pardonnez-moi*. She does a quick laugh-snort and shakes her head.

3:45 p.m. Bell goes, and I'm outta here. I'm a streak of lightning, dude. I'm faster than the World Curry Eating Champion speeding to the Gents, man.

The town's main shopping street is a short diversion from my normal route home. I head for Woolies, for the front left corner of the shop, past the special-offer DVDs, past the blank tapes, past the albums, to the CD singles rack.

Where is it? Where is it? . . .

Gotta be here, gotta be here. . . .

I'm scanning for that singer's face, or the word Plastic, or just something labeled, "Look! It's Here!" in five-meter neon letters with a pointy-finger arrow.

Wheresit, wheresit. . . .

There! Half a dozen copies, stacked at the No. 4 slot. No. 4? It's selling already! Oh, bless the distribution systems of major high street retailers!

All four members of Plastic look out at me from the cover, with the singer in front. They're all wearing black and standing against a swirly gray-black background. There's a small, brightly glowing love heart perched on her sleeve, like a bird of prey perched on its handler's glove. Underneath, simply: *Plastic 100% Love*, in a warped-looking typeface.

That's their typeface, their logo. I have a feeling I'll be seeing a lot of it from now on.

I pick up a copy from the rack and feel a certain swell of contentment. After all, I'm not just buying this single for me, I'm buying it for them too. To do my bit to help their fledgling careers, to show my support, that kind of thing.

It makes me feel like I'm a part of them, a part of what they do. A very tiny part, admittedly, but it's the principle that counts, isn't it?

That single goes straight into the portable CD player at home, with the Repeat button pressed. There are three different mixes of the one track, each as wonderful as the others.

I boogie around the house. I boogie around Gran. She giggles. I boogie around Grandad's chair. He looks bemused and just a little bit worried. I boogie around my tea. (Gran's patent pasta mushroom-y thing.) It doesn't make it taste any better. (Gran follows recipes by looking at the picture—to the eye, delicious; to the tongue, boiled socks. Makes you want to cry really.)

When Mum gets home, and then especially when Dad gets

home, the Repeat button suddenly wins this year's Most Fiendish Invention Ever Devised by the Mind of Man. I relocate my personal disco up to my room.

And thus it begins, my journey into the heart of Plastic. With this one CD, this one style-heavy cover design, this typeface.

With the music throbbing in the air, I slide the CD cover out from under those little curved bits that hold it in. I read through all the microprint on the back, looking for clues. All songs by Voyd/Parkins Copyright © Cellophane Music Ltd Unauthorized copying hiring lending public performance blah blah yum te tum. Plastic are: Sean Appleby, keyboards, Kurt Bartrom, drums, Mike Parkins, guitars, Lisa Voyd, lead vocals.

Her name is Lisa Voyd. And she writes the lyrics too!

I've never really been a FAN of something before. Not actually a FAN, as such. I've loved a particular song, or a particular CD, or a particular video, but I've never quite had that sort of attachment to an actual band.

I suppose what I mean is, I never felt like I was part of a gang. No, that's the wrong word. Part of a MOVEMENT! That's it. It feels like there's a swirling, shining wind of change sweeping right at you, sweeping over everyone, and you're inside it. It feels like there's something that transcends you, that goes beyond whatever you are, that is great and whole and good. Great, because when it all comes together it's so much more than all its individual pieces. Whole, because you're a part of it and if you weren't, then both you and it would be diminished. Good, because at its core is pure talent and skill, like you know you'll never have yourself.

You can't be like pop stars, but you can be part of their story. You can be their fan.

And I am a fan of Plastic. From that day forth, I'm one of the inner circle. I'm one of the select few who can proudly show you their complete collection of Plastic's music. I can hold you spellbound with my detailed knowledge of the band and its history.

I suppose pop music means different things to different people. It's a form of artistic expression, if you're that way inclined. Or it's a release of emotions, if you're the sort who doesn't otherwise release their emotions much. Or it's part of an ongoing tradition, if you're interested in social history, with its musical roots in old rock 'n' roll, or punk, or rap, or disco.

To me, Plastic is a badge to be worn with pride. Plastic is a tribe, and there are tribal looks and tribal beliefs. I've never really felt that kind of brotherhood before.

I've developed a kind of sixth sense. I've become alert to Plastic, the same way you're alert to your own name when you hear it against a load of background chatter. I home in on relevant words or pictures when I'm standing in front of the long bank of newspapers and magazines in WHSmith. I record stuff on TV on the off chance that there'll be something new mentioned, and I skip through the unwanted bits on fast forward.

Life takes on a whole new flavor. It's as if I've existed on bread and water all my life and now I'm in a Chinese restaurant having Szechuan vegetables and dim sum put in front of me. It all makes the everyday drag through the mud a lot more bearable. Everything now comes with tinted filters over the lens. You can put up with the crap because you know it doesn't matter, not compared to the important things in life, anyway. School and home and work and weekends all become accompanied by music. There's something for all occasions. Plastic to cheer me up when my day is bad. Plastic to sing along with when my day is good. There's always a track to be found that's relevant to what's going on. It's the soundtrack to my life.

Everything is so much better when coated in Plastic.

"Get up! He's standing!
Get up! She's demanding!
Get up! We're expanding
Our horizons"

—"No Kidding," from the Plastic album *More Sinned Against Than Sinning*
(Voyd/Parkins © Cellophane Music Ltd)

My nickname at school is Sherlock. As nicknames go, it's perfectly acceptable. At primary school I was generally called Bog Brush, for reasons I'm not even going to begin to explain, so Sherlock was a definite step up the nickname ladder. I suppose partly it's down to the Holmesian air of detachment I tend to cultivate. I'm one of those people who stay on the circumference of all the social circles, a member of each but never at the center. Which suits me fine. But mostly the Sherlock label is all about my powers of deduction.

I got the nickname in Year Seven, after I correctly worked out who'd been nicking software from the Computer lab. But any fool would have realized it was Manky Milo. The clincher was the way his body language changed—someone like that doesn't go from whopping younger kids on the head at every opportunity to standing nicely to attention with his arms innocently tucked into his blazer pockets. Well, not in the space of a week, anyway.

Of course, once you've got a reputation like that, you can

reinforce it even by noticing things that are really obvious. Now and again I'll tell someone at school that I know they took a shock-gasp illegal shortcut across the sports field this morning, or that they clearly haven't spent enough time on their history project, and they look at me as if I'm psychic. Then I explain just how really obvious it is to spot things from the state of their shoes or the entries on their library card, and they STILL look at me like I'm psychic.

You know, you can tell a lot from shoes. The new English teacher who started last term, for instance. I guessed that he'd recently left a job in journalism from what he was wearing, including his shoes.

(Age: mid-thirties, therefore has had a previous career. Manner: nervy, therefore new to teaching. Shoes: chunky, comfy, but rather worn, therefore a chap who's spent a lot of time out and about on his feet. Suit and tie: not new, but deliberately neat and unobtrusively dark, therefore someone probably used to assuming a professional appearance. Could be an ex–sales rep, but the choice of subject, English, suggests a more literary background. Deciding factor: pen movements during note-taking shows he knows shorthand. Most likely local employment possibility: journalism.)

He gaped at me openmouthed, and so did the rest of the class, when I explained my reasoning. Emma was impressed. Anyway, I'm telling you all this because it was my Sherlock tendencies that got me, Tanya and Tim better seats at the one and only concert Plastic ever played at the National Exhibition Center in Birmingham.

Tanya had declared her love for all things Plastic very soon after their first single came out. Well, to be more specific, she declared her love for all things Sean Appleby and from there her devotion spread from keyboard player to whole band.

She's an Amazon, is Tanya, and I'm not talking online retailers. You read about these warrior women of the dim and distant past and you can easily imagine someone like Tanya leading from the front, spear in hand, issuing bloodcurdling yells as she guts another antelope. Or whatever the Amazons ate. Which is all very odd, because the very thought of issuing a bloodcurdling yell, let alone eating an antelope, would send Tanya into spasms of girly horror.

As girls go, you see, Tanya is the girliest of girly girls. She makes pink pom-poms look brutal and masculine. It's just that her girliness isn't matched by her physique.

She's tall and broad-shouldered, with a shoe size which makes most of the Year Twelve rugby team look like five-year-olds. It's the perfect body for a champion swimmer, proven by the fact that one of her almost-identical older sisters IS a champion swimmer. However, Tanya absolutely hates swimming and gets in a right strop every time one of the school sports staff asks her to reconsider her position on the subject. The conversation normally goes something like:

Sports Staff Person: You'd be a natural, Tanya! It's good exercise, it's fun and you'd be contributing to the greater glory of the school!

Tanya: I'd be immersed in water that had been used by toddlers and old people! They don't call them public baths for nothing, you know, sir. The very idea is disgusting.

Sports Staff Person: There's chlorine in it. It's sanitized. You can smell how sanitized it is.

Tanya: And exactly how sanitary am I supposed to feel, sir, when some old lady's corn plaster comes bobbing along past my nose?

Sports Staff Person has no answer to that, admits defeat and retires to the staff room weeping openly into his mug of coffee.

Tanya's room at home is a shrine to data retrieval. Books, magazines, newspaper clippings, downloaded Web pages, you name it, it's there. And 85.2% of it is devoted to the study of Plastic. You will NEVER get the better of Tanya when it comes to organizing factual information. She's has a positive genius for it.

I've got a good few posters on my walls, but every square millimeter of her wallpaper is accounted for. You can't see the purple stripes at all anymore. She won't let either of her older sisters into her room now, not since one of them (the swimmer) splashed something fizzy on the rare picture that she had glue-sticked next to her light switch (from *Pop Hits* magazine, July, pull-out center pages).

It's Tanya who acts as official archivist for Tim's Plastic fan Web site, which he runs from his mum's PC. Tim is someone I only knew by sight until he joined the great and noble brotherhood of Plastic. The fact that he'd sat behind me in English and physics, in front of me in maths and next to me in geography for a term and a half had completely passed me by. I mean, he's a very nice bloke, when you get to know him—sharp as a pin, bit of a technical whiz, quite philosophical in his own way—he just isn't someone who stands out from a crowd.

Tim is a little bit freckly, a little bit round, a little bit short. Lots of little bits, basically. The sort of person who has mildness and moderation hardwired into all parts of his genetic structure. Or, at least, all parts of his genetic structure except the parts which control his sinuses. Those parts have concentrated all their little bits into one major long-term health project. The kid is a martyr to nasal congestion, a virtuoso on the catarrh. I get bouts of sneezing and itchy eyes myself, when the pollen count peaks, but Tim's nose harbors a collection of conditions which add up to keep mucus production at maximum 24/7: a little bit virus, a little bit hay fever, a little bit sinusitis.

You know when he's about because you can hear the membranous rustle of his supermarket bag as he walks. He's got a quick-march, eyes down, knees out way of walking which makes the carrier bag slap against the side of his leg all the time. You'd think it would drive him barmy, but he doesn't appear to notice it. Everything goes in a supermarket bag: schoolbooks, gym clothes, Plastic CDs, decongestant spray. I suppose there's no avoiding it: he's a bit of a nerd, really. To be brutally honest.

But I guess that's one of the nice things about Plastic fandom. It is, as you might say, a broad church. You get bog-standard types like me, you get nerds like Tim, you get kids, you get grungy teens, you get happy-dippy teens (you even get the occasional elderly person—for example, couples in their thirties). Emma, by the way, is not among the legion of fans. Silly girl doesn't know what she's missing.

So Tim, Tanya and I, the Three Plastic-eers, get to Birmingham International station at 7:10 p.m. on the evening of Friday 22 August. We hustle out of the packed train and join the steady streams of people heading for the NEC. Fast-flowing streams, spilling up the station stairs, defying gravity, surging. Bemused trickles of train travelers heading for the airport separate out from the fans and run the other way.

We're going to see them for the first time. They'll be in the SAME PLACE as us!

Nothing diverts the streams. Babbling brooks of badges, T-shirts, hair tied up like Lisa's in the "Happy Clappy" video. We're all strangers; we don't know each other's names and we don't know how far anyone else has come to get to this point, right here, right now, but we all know what's going on in everyone else's head. We all share something on the inside, and it's the weirdest feeling. Our faces don't mean a thing, but our thoughts are joined in a strange, intimate way that's half exciting and half peculiar.

Streams join into a river on the broad, enclosed walkway that crosses over the top of the railway lines. Tim, Tanya and I go with the flow over the tracks, down the other side, cutting a valley around the vast hangarlike sheds of the NEC. Closer every step.

Tanya lets out a burst of a squeal. "We're going to see them, we're going to see them."

Tim's face suddenly explodes in raw grin. "Yeah, yeah, yeah, yeah."

We all chant our individual mantra. We just can't help it. Our feet skip to the beat that's growing inside us. We're going to see them.

We're through the outer doors, with our tickets grasped tight and our stomachs feeling even tighter. And I spot something, not exactly out of the corner of my eye, but certainly way over stage left.

Across the shifting river-queue of people, ahead of us, nearly at the ticket checkers, there's a man who's changing his mind. I catch quick vertical glimpses of him as fans move about between him and me. He's built like a bulldog, and dressed in a double-breasted suit which in itself marks him out as someone who isn't entirely comfortable here. His hair looks like it wants to be on a different head; it's gelled and forced into a rough sea on the top, like a badly iced cake. He looks like a Cockney wide boy.

He turns, looking around himself awkwardly, and I see he's got a hideous lime green tie that'd drown out the music if you let it anywhere near the band. I reckon he's a friend of a friend of someone in telly or radio, the sort of business contact who gets the occasional perk as a sweetener. Whatever, he's here on a freebie. And so are his friends.

They're more difficult to read. A woman in a red dress, the cut of which I recognize from a magazine Emma at school insisted on showing me a while ago: designer, smart, violently expensive. And there's another man, younger than the exec, and the exact opposite of the woman in that he looks like he's dressed in Yves Saint Rubbish Tip. Colleagues, maybe? Girlfriend and "business associate"? Anyway, that part doesn't matter. What matters is what these two DO have in common. They're both drunk. Not falling over, stupid-pathetic, throwing up drunk, but unfocused, need-a-steady-hand, trying-too-hard-to-stay-still drunk.

They won't let them in. The thought hits me like a cup of cold water in the face. I bet she's got a bottle of something in that handbag, too. It's heavy. She's holding it oddly.

Mr. Wide Boy wants an excuse to go. He's been given three tickets and he's thought: Oh well, it's cost me nuffin', I might as well. And then he's chosen exactly the wrong people to invite along. He can't have connections too high up the executive ladder, or he wouldn't be in the queue with the rest of us, but even so . . .

Sure enough, the brick walls in sweatshirts and baseball caps who are checking tickets hold the three of them back. Ask a few questions. I can't hear them above the chatter of the crowd, but what they're saying is clear enough. What's in the bag, madam? Have you been having a drink, sir? Sorry, you're not coming in. No, sorry. No, I don't believe you, madam, sorry. It's health and safety. We've got every right, sir. It's not me making a berk of myself, sir. Move aside, please, you're holding everyone up here.

Mr. Wide Boy steers the pair of them away quickly. The expression on his face ought to appear in a textbook, labeled: *Fifty percent irritation, fifty percent embarrassment.* Make your move, I think to myself. Nothing ventured, nothing gained. If you don't ask, you don't get. The squeaky wheel gets the oil. The two embarrassments pass by muttering at each other, their faces bouncing around like a tennis match with too many balls. Mr. Wide Boy sweeps along behind them, out of my reach. I step out of the queue and touch his shoulder as he draws level with me. Tanya and Tim suddenly make a grab for me, thinking I've been hijacked or something.

"What now?" grunts Mr. Wide Boy.

"I'm sorry to bother you, but I couldn't help noticing how irritating and embarrassing your colleagues have been and since your tickets were complimentary—"

"How on earth did you know that?"

"—I thought I'd appeal to your good nature. My friends and I are huge Plastic fans, but we're also impoverished students, and if you'd like to turn your evening around by making three people enormously grateful and happy . . ." I give a shrug, to say "can we have your tickets" as meekly as possible.

He laughs like a donkey. "You cheeky young sod," he says with a broad smile.

We sit about thirty meters closer to the stage than we would have been. We're now about twenty meters back, over to the side.

"You're a genius, Dom," says Tanya. She pulls me over to her by the collar and lands a smacker on my cheek. Tim starts fidgeting and points out the lighting rigs and what kind of power surge it'll cause in the local substation when they're switched on.

Before the main event, an anonymous support band comes on and insults our ears with forty-five minutes of forgettable rubbish.

"How DARE they put these people on the same bill as Plastic!" cries Tanya, above the noise.

"Maybe they're just here to make Plastic look good?" suggests Tim.

Tanya shifts round in her seat to face him. "Plastic are quite capable of looking good by themselves!"

Tim mentally slaps himself on the forehead. "Yup. Of course. You're right." After a couple of minutes he comes up with a way to redeem himself. "I've had to exclude six users from the forum section of the Web site. They wouldn't stop posting things saying the new album's not as good as the first. Apparently some of the other main sites have had the same thing."

"People like that want locking up," says Tanya. Tim furrows his brow and gives a couple of firm nods. "Oh God," says Tanya, "Trackerman wasn't one of them, was he?"

"Oh no no no no!" says Tim. "No, no way."

"I bet he's here somewhere," I say, doing a quick scan of the audience. "He's from Wolverhampton, isn't he?"

"So his registration e-mail said." Tim nods, scraping at his nose with his crumpled hanky. "But you can't be sure, can you? I thought about sending out a bot to pinpoint his IP address, but you don't know the data wouldn't end up in the wrong hands. If I blew his cover I'd never live with myself."

Trackerman is a prince among fans at the moment. He's edited himself into thirty seconds of footage from the "Happy Clappy" video and posted it on half a dozen sites. There he is, strutting his stuff with Lisa Voyd. The guy must have some fabulous computer kit at home. Fantastic piece of work. It's getting whoops of glee from fans worldwide, apparently. Plastic's lawyers are after him, of course.

Tanya's neck and shoulders are twitching to a tune that's got nothing to do with what's going on up onstage. Her long hair is tied up and bobbing. "It's absolutely outrageous," she says. "How can anyone seriously think *From Hell It Came* is better than the new album? They're both equal works of genius, for God's sake."

We get on to the subject of album titles. *From Hell It Came* is an ironic take on an old 1950s B-movie.

"Yes, everyone knows that," says Tanya.

"But *More Sinned Against Than Sinning* isn't a movie title, is it?" says Tim.

"Not that I've ever heard of," I say.

"I think it's a comment on their treatment by the media," says Tanya, pursed lips wrinkling her lipstick. "I mean, they make so much up and get so many things wrong, it must be maddening for the whole band. Last week's *ChartLife* printed that Lisa's favorite ice cream flavor is vanilla, and Kurt's best moment was signing their record deal, and NEITHER of those is right. I mean, what are they playing at?"

I lean over to her. "What if they were right and you're wrong?"

She slaps me on the arm. "I am not wrong! I cross-check and verify from at least two or three sources, and I am not wrong!"

"The point is," says Tim, "that you are our definitive reference point. As long as we've got you to sort the truth from the lies, then we'll be OK, won't we?" I wonder whether he's half joking, but he seems perfectly sincere.

Tanya flicks him a couple of appreciative looks, then holds his face in her hands for a moment and gives his cheeks a hug. "Aww, thanks, Tim."

Tim is extremely pleased with himself, then extremely self-conscious, then extremely pleased with himself again. His eyes move like he's following a fly.

"Tim, what do you think, then, about my numerology theory?" says Tanya. "I don't normally take much notice of things like that, but I got the current *Fashion & You* because there was a thing about Lisa's hair in it, and there was an article about numerology. It said how you get numerical connections in life, and I suddenly spotted something. Lisa, Sean, Kurt, Mike, they've all got four letters. I reckon that could be really significant."

"Hmm," says Tim, his eyebrows not sure what positions to adopt.

"Naah, rubbish," I pipe up. "Mike is Michael. That's seven letters, it doesn't work."

"Ah!" says Tanya, holding up a manicured finger for emphasis. "But he chose to be known as Mike. Not Michael, or Mikey, but Mike. That's the significant bit. Maybe they're all linked by fate. They were destined to form this band."

"Still rubbish," I say.

"Perhaps you should keep looking for other significant numbers?" says Tim hopefully. "You know, back the theory up. More evidence."

The support band have gone. There's a low murmur across the

ocean of audience, like whale song, calling to fans. Last week we were days away from this moment, then hours, then minutes, and now it's here. There's a rumble of expectation, a speeding up of breath, thousands of eyes fixed ahead. They're going to be here. They're going to be here any second now.

Lights at the back of the stage slowly glow into life, red, green, blue, bringing monumental, curtainlike set designs out of the shadows. For the first time, we can see tall banks of video screens at the back, arranged into columns. They flick into life—soundless, snowy static at first, then single colors which twist together into the logo, sideways, draped up each video column like fluttering medieval banners. Everywhere is gloom, except the stage.

We edge to the front of our seats. We can feel our pulses bumping through us. I think my hand is shaking. I pull it into a fist. If only Emma were here, she'd understand the Plastic world.

A voice booms out of the semidarkness. Steady and low.

"Ladies and gentlemen . . . Will you please welcome to the stage . . . PLASTIIIIIIC!"

A howling, thundering roar erupts around us. A huge, magnificent yell of thousands and thousands of voices. Arms fly up. In the same instant, flashes crackle across the stage, hurling glittering clouds of light in a giant arc.

And there they are.

KAA-KLOOOOOWWW!

The first bar of "100% Love" throbs through us. A second wave of cheers breaks against the stage. Lisa Voyd steps forward, with logo-splashed T-shirt and thick-soled sneakers, microphone in hand. My insides feel like they've turned into pure light.

She's at the very edge of the stage. "Hello! Nice to see ya! Now SING!"

And we sing.

We know every word and every note of every song. The insistent pop drumbeat, the cascading melodies, the heart-thrilling unexpected mesh of instruments and tones. This is the Plastic sound.

Now and again, Tanya and Tim and I cast a quick look at each other. It's a way of showing ourselves that all this is real. Here we are, the three of us, with eyes a-shining and minds aglow, together with a few thousand friends and the greatest group in the history of popular music.

And the most wonderful moment of all is almost at the end. The cheers and whoops subside before the intro to "I Heart You" starts up. It's the slowest, moodiest track on the new album. For a second or two there's just Mike Parkins strumming out that sad and beautiful tune, and then . . .

Even before Lisa can begin, there's a couple of dozen voices, out there in the dark, beginning it for her.

And two dozen become a hundred, and then all of us, every last one of us, join in too, merging to a single, united sound.

Tears stream down Tanya's face, but somehow she's not crying. There's a ballooning pride and joy in all of us, a feeling so huge we can barely contain it, and it shines in the faces of the band, and in Lisa's especially. She sings the last verse with us.

40

Then there are bows, and yells, and whistles, and waves, and lights, and chatter, and stairs, and doors, and a platform, and a train. We keep looking at each other all over again. We smile and giggle and don't say a word. Nothing needs to be said.

A while later, we're walking down the steep path that leads from the station. The last red-orange rays of light are sliding sleepily behind the houses across the main road. It's been a dank summer, but tonight the air is clean and warm. The trees that line the path are absolutely still, and above them the sky glides cloudlessly through a freshly washed spectrum.

Dad's due to pick us up from the station, but he's not here yet. We cross the road and go into the brightly lit rectangle of the chip shop. Chips are just doing, be ready in a few minutes, OK?

We sit on the wide, tiled windowsill, backs to the glass. There are some moments you feel like you'll remember forever. Rare, still moments when everything is NOW, as if everything has been stopped and hushed so that you can take it all in. When things are just as they should be, and everyone is on your side, and the whole world makes sense. I'm sitting on that ledge, with my fellow fans, with the hairy bloke in his fat-stained white apron shoveling chips behind the counter, with the big, round clock on the wall and the slab of kebab meat turning on its vertical spit. Suddenly, there's peace, perfection, happiness. In that one, tiny moment of time.

"Nothing on your face, no shiny window in your eye, No thread of hair can ever change, I love you as you are"

—"I Heart You," from the Plastic album *More Sinned Against Than Sinning* (Voyd/Parkins © Cellophane Music Ltd)

12:58 p.m. We have now been stuck in the lift for thirty-one minutes.

Lisa sighs and shakes her head slowly. "*More Sinned Against Than Sinning* is a quote from *King Lear*, you dipstick!"

Out of everything I've just told her, that's the bit she picks on. "What, Shakespeare?" I say.

"Of course Shakespeare! How many *King Lear*s are there?"

The air in the lift is starting to feel humid. The hard surface of the floor is making my backside ache. I shuffle uncomfortably.

"Well," I say, "Tanya's never turned that fact up in *ChartLife*."

"Oh really? You don't say!"

A pang of some-feeling-or-other about Lisa scrapes across me, and it's not my usual disco mix of admiration and respect. I look down through the glass. Tim and Tanya are still there, standing their ground. They're getting jostled on all sides but they're not budging an inch. Tanya's holding onto the back of a Special Offers CD rack to stop the push of the crowd overbalancing her.

There are several security guards in sight, arms outstretched, issuing orders with hand gestures to stand back, stand still, no pushing there. I can't understand why they've not cleared the shop. I don't pick up any clues from them about that. As I was an hour ago, when I entered the shop, I'm puzzled by how limited they are in numbers.

The Big Deal Records staff are milling about in their yellow T-shirts, looking lost. A couple of them have put on dark glasses, in order to look as menacing as the security guards.

The fan in the bright green pullover is still pointing his video camera up at me. He pauses now and again to take shots of the guards. He also takes shots of the three TV crews who are positioned as far inside the shop as the guards will allow them. The TV crews have got cameras that are three times the size of the fan's, plus portable lights, plus reporters, plus satellite uplinks. But he's the one closer to the action. He's the one getting the better pictures.

The balding store manager with the ID badge seems to have calmed down a bit. He's continuing to keep his nails freshly chewed, though. When they're not being chewed, the fingers of his right hand keep fluttering around the leather-encased phone clipped to his waistband, like he's waiting to use it.

The knot of ten-year-old girls in Plastic sweatshirts have stopped flipping through the racks and have chosen a handful of CDs each. They're squeezing their way through to the sales counter.

"Who's this Emma you keep mentioning?"

I turn back to Lisa. She's taking the cover off her phone and picking at its innards. The level of her voice reminds me just how little outside sound is getting in.

"I don't keep mentioning Emma," I say. For some reason the words come out all defensive.

"Yes you do. She must be important to you."

"No she isn't. She's just a friend at school."

"I see."

I've known Emma Lawrence since our first day at secondary school. I discovered that the previous year she'd broken her leg on a school trip (to a zoo! It's a long story). She'd missed the last part of the summer term, so I offered to help her catch up on various subjects, which is how we got friendly in the first place.

Emma Lawrence is the blondest person I know. I don't mean she's blond in the sense of ditzy—she doesn't go around in a T-shirt with "Natural Blonde: Please Speak Slowly" on it. I mean her hair is the kind of perfectly even light straw color than would give Barbie a hissy fit of jealousy. She considers it a hindrance.

"I might as well have an eye patch or a terrible facial deformity. It's the only way people pick me out. Emma? Oh yes, the girl with the hair."

I pull an aww-shucks face at her and carry on eating my delicious and nutritious school lunch. "If it's that bad, just dye it."

She lets out a long sigh. "Nah. It's the only way people pick me out."

She says contradictory things like that all the time. She's the only person I know who can hold eight different opinions on the same subject, and believe all of them at once.

Emma is a walking paradox. She's very intelligent—she and I battle it out for the top-of-the-class slot unceasingly—but I will never, EVER understand how her mind works. Never. To me, her inner thoughts are a maze of conflicting mental processes. On the inside: arrgh! On the outside: serenity. And there's the paradox.

It's not that we don't get on. We get on very well—we have the same silly sense of humor, we're often sniggering over something which leaves everyone else baffled. Sometimes we have running jokes over things that happen, so that weeks later one of us only has to say a particular word and it sets us both off again.

The word that springs to most people's minds when they meet Emma is "compact." She's not tall. Not short . . . just, not tall. Her height is one of the hundred thousand things you shouldn't poke fun at her over. Not unless you want a kick on the shin.

She has a long, high-cheekboned face, with the sort of mouth which permanently looks like it's about to kiss a small child, and steely blue eyes which turn into ice sculptures whenever we're locked in debate. She's always immaculately dressed. She has the neatest, most snag-free, most colorfast school uniform in the entire world, and an out-of-school wardrobe that would make a hard-nosed business executive look shabby.

As a look, it's not exactly rock chick. Lisa Voyd, she ain't.

Her ambition is to be a concert pianist. I kid you not. Not that there's anything wrong with concert pianists per se, but it strikes me as a rather dull ambition, that's all. It's one of the many things about which we have our regular verbal jousting matches. When on the subject of classical piano music I use expressions like "middle-aged" and "old-fashioned" and she uses expressions like "artistic savage" and "ignorant pig-boy."

I think she gets her lack of hip and trendiness from her parents. They're both doctors: her dad is an educational psychologist (just what the world needs—more eggheads reminding you that school is a madhouse), and her mum is a polli-globa-something-or-other-ist. I can never remember exactly what, it's all livers and spleens and stuff; utterly hideous. She has an older sister who's also a doctor, who lives in London and whom I've never met. You might think, with so many subscribers to the *British Medical Journal* in the family, that Emma's parents would be a bit sniffy or disappointed in their younger daughter's career of choice. Not a bit of it. They're the most infuriatingly calm, pleasant, supportive, rational people you could ever hope to meet. After ten minutes in their company all I want to do is scream. OK, so it's just gnawing jealousy on my part, I admit. With a family like mine, can you blame me?

The Lawrences live in an intimidatingly nice house two streets the other side of the school playing field. Three things it doesn't have: (1) grubby marks on the carpets, (2) half an inch of dust on every flat surface higher than two meters off floor level, (3) resident grandparents.

What does MY house have? All of the above! The grubby marks

are due to having a little brother in the house who is permanently on the point of reverting to mankind's Neanderthal origins. The dust is due to having parents who have "demanding" jobs (one of those demands being, so it appears, that they ignore the cupboard with all the cleaning stuff in). The grandparents speak for themselves. Gran is still in the grip of the hippie fashions of 1971. Grandad definitely isn't. Grandad's wardrobe thinks it's still 1958. I really wish that Mum would have the guts to tell her father that gel applied to just a few dozen remaining hairs is not only a waste of time but does actually still need to be washed off occasionally.

Nominally, Gran does the cleaning around the house, but since her idea of a thorough sanitizing is two flicks with a damp cloth followed by tea and biscuits, not a lot gets done. Besides, her stumpy legs stop her reaching anything higher than the top of the telly.

Admittedly, there are a lot of surfaces to dust. The rooms in our house are pretty average size-wise, but they contain enough furniture and bric-a-brac to stock a moderately impressive chain of antique shops. No, "antique" is the wrong description. What's the word I'm looking for? "Junk," that's the word.

Quite a bit of it came from Gran and Grandad's old house. They sold the house about five years ago and moved to Spain. Then they decided they didn't want to live in Spain after all. So they moved in with us, and the entire contents of their old house moved back from Spain with them.

The official reason they moved in with us was a combination of their age, their health and how you could never get proper tea on the Continent. You can adjust the emphasis from one factor to another according to how much Grandad's leg is playing him up today. The unofficial reason is that, with us two pesky kids around, having our grandparents in the house for the fourteen hours a day that our parents *aren't* made sense in lots of ways.

What with one thing and another, it's amazing that I've turned out as sensible and well-balanced as I am. Seb is a lost cause. His idea of fun is digging for dinosaur bones in the garden and then winding Mum and Dad up about it later.

Seb: But Mum, Dad said I could dig out the shrubs!
Mum: What? Dad! What did you tell him that for?
Dad: I didn't! Seb, don't tell lies!
Seb: I'm NOT! Mum, he told me! (*Tears well up expertly in eyes*)
Mum: Oh, for God's sake, Dad!
Dad: He's lying! Sebastian, tell Mummy the truth!
Seb: He did tell me, Mum! (*Nodding head earnestly*)
Gran: Does anybody want a biscuit?
Dad: Seb! You know what I think about liars!
Mum: Dad! Don't speak to him like that! It's bad enough we're not here for the children as it is, without you undermining his confidence!
Dad: Oh, and I get in from work later than you, then, do I?

And so on. My parents run on guilt the same way toys run on batteries. I much prefer it when they're at work. I can get some peace and quiet. The only exception to that rule is at weekends, when Dad takes over the cooking from Gran. He can cook. She can't. We spend weekdays as hunter-gatherers on the vast open spaces of the fridge.

It's made worse by the fact that Gran and Grandad do the shopping. At three, every Monday afternoon, come rain, shine or natural disaster. It's set in stone. It's in their itinerary, it's part of their unchanging weekly routine.

Every Monday afternoon at half past four, they unpack the eight carrier bags. There are always eight. Trust me. Out onto the kitchen table come the Usual Purchases, which include: the tiny scented bar of soap wrapped in the sheet of newspaper Gran takes with her ("It stops the smell getting in the food!"); the *el cheapo* economy bread, which tastes like the tiny scented bar of soap; and the packet of cornflakes put into two layers of bag in case those deadly sharp corners should rip their way to freedom and have somebody's eye out.

"Graaaan!" I say. "These things under the cornflakes are nearly thawed. They've got meat in them; they shouldn't be refrozen. They can harbor dangerous bacteria."

"I've never poisoned anybody yet with me cooking," she says, popping the plastic-wrapped cheese under the cheese-shaped china cover in the fridge.

I don't know why I let myself get drawn into these pointless discussions with Gran, I really don't. She waddles across to the kettle, the unironed frills on the hem of her long skirt billowing.

"Eee, I'm cream-crackered," she sighs. She yells through to the living room. "Seednee, d'you want some tea, lovey?"

We wait for the statutory three seconds while Grandad composes himself. "N'h," he grunts quietly. "Think me tummy's playing up."

"Please yourself," she mumbles happily. You'd think her insides would have liquefied, with the amount of tea she sloshes down.

It's on account of my family being such a bunch of walking horrors that I try to avert any contact between them and the real world as much as possible. Unfortunately, stuff like Parents' Evenings and school social get-togethers tend to make things difficult in that department. I damn that accursed PTA and all its hellish home-school link programs!

It was at a Parents' Evening that Mum and Dad met Emma's parents. Naturally, I'd made sure I wasn't there. It was the one occasion when my usual aww-shucks-so-much-homework-so-little-time strategy for staying at home turned out to be the wrong approach to the problem.

How they all got talking, I shall never know. But they did. And from that point on, Mum and Dad start holding up Emma in front of me like some Angel of Virtue. "The Lawrences are such nice people," says Mum. "You ought to ask Emma over sometime."

"No, Mum."

Or . . . "That Emma's already given a lot of thought to her future career," says Dad. "You ought to start giving some thought to your future career."

"Zip it, Dad."

Notice, however, that Mum and Dad never mix with the Lawrences socially, except at school functions. My mum ring Emma's mum for a girly chat? You gotta be kidding. Emma's dad invite my dad for a drink down the pub? Not in a million years. It's one of the Great Unwritten Rules among adults: Yea verily, if thy neighbor doth have a nicer house and a higher disposable income than thou, thou shalt consider thyself slightly inferior in all ways, and thy neighbor shall agree with thee. Pathetic, if you ask me, but at least it means I can keep Emma confined to school and away from the freaks who populate my home. It's not that I care about what she thinks of me or my family, you understand. It's simply that they're so embarrassing. I don't like to even acknowledge they're mine.

I'm pretty certain that Emma's parents have never held ME up in front of HER as an ideal to aspire to! So her continued attempts to advise and improve me are just plain irritating. She seems to have that annoying desire to "mold" me that some girls exhibit towards their . . . I was about to say "boyfriends" but that's hardly the word I'm looking for! I suppose MOST girls who have that molding-their-men tendency require the target of their molding to have formed some sort of emotional attachment to them before they begin. Not Emma. She's obviously happy to mold even the least moldable of friends. Like me.

Case in point: my birthday last year. Emma and I get on OK, as I said, so we're pally enough to give each other birthday pressies. It's a bit like when you get a fictional character and their archnemesis trying to outdo each other most of the time, then stopping here and there to slap each other on the back. "Aha! You are a worthy opponent, Baron Von Dastardly!" "As are you, Sir Hero, but I shall still do better in the exams than you! On guard!"

Emma gets me concert tickets. Which was very nice of her. What's slightly less nice was that they're tickets to a classical music concert at the Symphony Hall. She knows I've never paid much attention to that sort of thing. We "debate" about it all the time.

"So it's time to change your mind," she says, smiling and raising her eyebrows at me.

We're taking our seats at the concert. It's a curvaceous, old-fashioned venue, all Greek columns and stone cherubs. The ceiling is a swirl of cornices and decorated ridges, with its low-domed background painted a deep crimson. The place must echo impressively until it's filled with enough people to deaden the effect, which tonight it most definitely is. Tiers of comfy, flip-down seats in a shade which matches the ceiling, elegant balconies which look like giant, emptied-out seashells glued to the walls. People are chatting, a low mumble of unconnected conversation warming up the atmosphere. Most of them are dressed neatly, in office-y suits or thin V-neck Marks & Sparks pullovers. Naturally, I'm in Plastic T-shirt and hooded fleece. Lisa Voyd's fabulous left eye beams out from my chest. Naturally, Emma gives my ensemble one of her try-as-you-might-you're-not-going-to-embarrass-me looks.

"Wouldn't hurt YOU to adopt a trendier sense of dress," I say. "After all, Lisa Voyd is the ideal example for womankind."

She zaps me one of her ice glares and a fixed grin. "I prefer to be my own person, thank you. I don't need to go around masquerading as a pop star. Wouldn't hurt YOU to be more individual."

"Are you trying to mold me again?"

She casts a quick hand gesture around the grandeur of the place. "I'm trying to open your eyes," she says. "One day, maybe, you'll realize that the world of classical music is—"

"The dreary, irrelevant rubbish I've always suspected it is."

She turns in her seat to face me. Her ultrablond hair does a shoosh around her head that wouldn't look out of place in a shampoo ad. "How much do you know about the construction of pop music?"

We appear to have made one of her illogical leaps again. "Huh?"

"How much do you know about the way pop music is actually put together, musically? Tempo, harmonies, rhythm, all that kind of thing. How much?"

One corner of my mouth does an I-don't-get-it squiggle. "I listen to it, Em. I don't play it."

"You're good at maths, aren't you?" she says, aiming a finger at me for emphasis.

Is she leading me into a verbal trap of some sort here, methinks? Hmm, can't see one coming, OK, I'll answer the question, m'lud. "Yeah, you know I am."

"Right," she says, with an air of having proved her point. "So you'd be good at musical theory. I struggle with it quite a lot, but you'd find it a breeze."

"You are trying to mold me, aren't you? For the zillionth time, I don't want to play the piano, OK? You might need to know all that stuff, but I don't."

"Nooo," she says, doing a little bounce of frustration in her seat.

"I mean . . ." She slumps down for a moment. "Look, you're always saying how passionate you are about Plastic, and the music you love, right?"

". . . Right."

"Right. But you don't take the trouble to find out about it, do you?"

I'm starting to get a bit cheesed off at this point. "There's barely anything about Plastic I haven't found out about." I point to my T-shirt. "Eee gee. Lisa Voyd. Born, fourth of June, Stourbridge. (So, local girl!) Went to Coten End Primary School, then to—"

"I don't mean that!"

"You're having a lot of trouble saying what you mean, here, Em."

"I am, aren't I! Fine. OK. Johann Sebastian Bach, born in Eisenach, Germany, the youngest son of Johann Ambrosius Bach . . ."

"What's Bach got to do with it?" I say.

Emma points to the tiered stage, where musicians are limbering up to begin. "You're about to hear something he composed? The St. John Passion?"

"Oooh! Right."

"The point is, Dom, we can all spout facts and statistics. It's all surface, isn't it? It's got no depth to it. How can you claim to have a passionate interest in something, and then make no effort to properly understand it?"

"Are you saying that classical music can't be understood unless you study it in depth?"

"I'm saying NOTHING can be properly understood unless you make the effort to understand it."

"Pop music is about emotion. It's not meant to be analyzed."

"Oh, and classical music contains no emotion?"

"Not in the same way, no."

A ripple of applause begins to swell. The conductor appears, gives a couple of minimal bows towards the audience and turns, arms raised.

Emma emits a noise that's half sigh, half snort. Her face looks very smooth in the warm-toned light, and her mouth is pressed as if words are fighting to get out. "For God's sake, Dominic, I . . . ," she says at last, lowering her voice as the applause subsides into silence. "You're the most intelligent, capable person I know, and you just . . . If you'd just TRY more, think what you'd accomplish."

I feel a bit huffy. She's molding me, that's all it is.

The music begins. I suppose it's OK. Not exactly exciting.

After about ten minutes I glance over at Emma. There's a shining tear poised at the top of her cheek. It kind of startles me. Maybe I was wrong about the emotion thing.

Lisa has listened to me carefully. Now, quietly, she says, "You're an idiot."

(1:14 p.m. Lift time elapsed: forty-seven minutes.)

There's a lot of "quietly" in here. I shuffle against the glass and the sound feels abnormally loud. Lisa raises her head, pressing her hair to the brushed metal of the back of the lift. She gives a sharp hum, quite high, and then after a short pause she begins to sing. Sing! And there's only me here!

I think it's in German. It definitely isn't anything that's currently nestling in my iPod.

She sings long, perfect notes, a flowing, aching sound that sets the very air on edge. I can't move, or make the slightest noise. All I can do is listen to this utterly beautiful sound. I'm suddenly aware of every square millimeter of myself, and the lift, and the glass, and everything, all of it shot through with this music that fills my mind from the inside out. And I know it from somewhere. Not like this, though, not in this crystal-clear vocal liquid.

Lisa stops midtune. She blinks a couple of times, and the movement is huge and slow, like theater curtains falling and rebounding. She looks at me.

"I know that from somewhere," I say. "It's beautiful."

"Of course you know it," she whispers. "Emma took you to hear it, idiot. It's from Bach's *St. John Passion*."

A stab of mental discomfort enters at the base of my brain. Who's holding the knife, I can't quite tell. It IS beautiful. Why didn't I see it that way at the concert?

"Sorry," I mumble. "That thing was ages ago. Wish I'd never gone now."

"Well, be grateful you did," says Lisa. "I absolutely adore that sort of music, and I never get to go to classical concerts anymore. Only an idiot wouldn't be pleased to get a birthday present like that."

The knife gets a good twist and I shuffle again. My bum appears to be in a coma. "Surely you can go to any concert you like?"

"You think?" she says, her gaze moving away from me.

"Well . . . If you don't get time, or something . . . I dunno, change your schedule."

"Simple as that," she says. "Change my schedule. Change everything. I wouldn't know where to begin."

"But if you—"

"Just. Shut! Up!"

"Admit it, boy, you like my skin
You wouldn't like what lurks within"

—"Double It Up," from the Plastic album *Highly Offensive*
(Voyd/Parkins © Cellophane Music Ltd)

It's about nine on a Sunday evening, and as I'm flopped out on
my bed reading through some seriously in-depth stuff about Plastic
that Tanya's found on the Web and printed out for me, there's a
knock at my door. Mum pokes her head in at handle level before I
can shout, "Go away, I'm doing a vital school project and mustn't be
disturbed for any reason whatsoever. This means you!"

She pauses for a second while her features compose themselves
into something that's meant to look casual. "Hi, Dominic, can I
come in?"

I flow a hand languidly towards the chair beside my desk. Mum
flashes me a smile so quick it barely exists, and perches on the chair.
There's a silence that couldn't be more uncomfortable if it were
filled with rusty nails.

"How are you, Dominic?"

"Fine. Why?"

"Well, no reason, just . . ." Her whole head does a birdlike twitch.

"It's just we haven't had a talk for a while, and I don't want you to think I'm not here to listen to anything you might want to say."

Oh God. A talk. "There's nothing I want to say, Mum."

"Because I am here. Anytime you do need to talk."

There's always a simple way to get rid of her at this point, but it's not without risk. There's a remark I can make. A rather cruel and insensitive remark, I have to admit, but it will either have the desired effect and send her scurrying back downstairs, or else (and this is the risk) it will make things worse and send her off down the "talking" route. I weigh up the pros and cons for a moment or two. I decide to take a chance.

"Except when you're at work, obviously."

"Sorry?"

"Yeh, of course, we can talk anytime. Except when you're out, obviously."

Moment of truth. Mum's eyebrows console each other with a hug, and she suddenly starts paying attention to the heap of stuff on my desk. "Dominic, I don't want you and Sebastian to think we don't love you."

Damn.

"Muuum, we don't think that, OK? You love us, we love you, right?"

Damn. Nothing I say will salvage the situation now. Mum's tongue starts pulling at her mouth as if it's trying to twang her lips across the room. I really don't need this.

"Because I know Dad and I have demanding jobs. It's just that we want to make sure you have all the things in life that . . . that some of us might not have had when we were growing up, you know? Growing up with your gran and grandad."

"Yes, Mum."

"But you mustn't mind that Dad is absent so much. Just because he's never here, doesn't mean . . . Of course, it would be nice if he could talk to you himself, now, with me, as agreed, but apparently IT systems demand more attention than a family. Still, please don't feel you can't come to us with problems, yes?"

"Yes, Mum."

"Are there any problems that are bothering you at the moment?"

"No, Mum."

"Because you can tell me, really you can."

"I know. There are no problems bothering me at the moment."

"Are you sure? Please tell me."

"There is nothing bothering me. I promise."

"Because I know being a teenager these days is very . . . Well, there are things in the world that . . . You would tell me if you had a problem, wouldn't you?"

"Yes, Mum." Please go away.

"Any sort of problem? I mean, with girls, or in school, or out of school—"

"Mum! For God's sake!"

She flashes the palms of her hands. "Yes, sorry, of course, you're right, you're a sensible boy, silly of me, I'm sorry."

OK. Can you go now? Apparently not.

Mum starts perusing the stuff on my desk. Most of it is Plastic. It clearly baffles her. "I don't think I've heard these ones, have I?"

"You probably have, Mum."

"All sound the same to me these days. They look quite nice, though, not like some of them. Some of them are a bit weird, aren't they." Silence. "What are you reading?"

"It's an article from *Celebrity Central*. About where the members of Plastic are buying houses."

"Oh. Right," she says brightly. I can see she's desperate to add, "That's a sensible investment, I approve of good financial role models for young people," but then thinks better of it. She reminds me about being here for me at all times of the day and night, then goes downstairs to watch something lifestyle-related on BBC3.

This meeting leaves me with a feeling of queasy unease. The sort of feeling that's covered in sticky labels saying, "This Is Inappropriate!" and "Uncomfortable Brush with Reality! Avoid! Avoid!" The sort of feeling you get when you realize that your parents really WERE teenagers once, or when the little old man next door mistakes you for his long-dead son.

It's the same feeling I'm left with when Lisa Voyd makes it clear what a squishable bug she thinks I am. I don't quite understand. What have I done to offend her? It's as if I were standing in front of the most impressive and spectacular building in the world, only to have it take one look at me and decide to collapse rather than let me admire it.

It hurts. It really hurts. If you'd told me, ten minutes before entering that lift, that shortly over an hour later I'd be finding Lisa rude, ill-tempered and hurtful, I'd be too busy sewing my split sides back together to express my disdain for you.

But . . .

There's something . . . amiss about her. Something sad and disjointed. I'm suddenly aware of the growing gap between the Dominic Smith version of Lisa Voyd and the Lisa Voyd version of Lisa Voyd. Until I got into the lift I assumed they were one and the same, but now they're drifting apart like melting icebergs.

I can't begin to untangle the knot of emotional barbed wire that's lodged itself in my head.

I know precisely what Emma would say. . . .

"Typical male, can't get in touch with his feelings."

"It's what being male is all about," I say, dolloping ketchup on the side of my plate.

Emma pauses while she gives her cutlery a vicious seeing-to with a paper serviette. "This canteen must buy its dishwashers at Useless Electrical Appliances 'R' Us," she grumbles. Then she returns to the matter in hand. "It's nothing to be proud of, Dom. The world would be a happier place if boys expressed themselves more."

"You mean if they were more like girls?" I say. Tim sniggers.

"No," says Emma calmly. "I mean if they were more aware of their emotions."

"Yeh. Like girls. That's the trouble with you women: you don't understand boys, so you want to girlify them."

"Oi!" says Tanya, through a mouthful of pie.

"A boy who's aware of his emotions is a more complete human being," says Emma.

"Yeh. And just a little bit girly."

Tim sniggers again. Tanya makes a huffy noise and digs at her pie.

The four of us have got a corner table. Lunchtime at school is mainly a scramble of legs, loose change and huge metal serving dishes, but if you're sneaky and get past Mrs. Grumpy the Till Goblin at the right time, you can find a quiet spot. We're at the small table right over by the far wall, next to the window, which is a place where you can catch the wintry draft coming from the outside but avoid the Year Sevens and teaching staff coming from the inside.

Emma's got her teeth into more than her tomato-pasta-thing now. "If boys are afraid to confront their emotions, that's their loss." I can see her sort of half-smirking at me. She knows perfectly well that I can't let that one go. She's poking at her pasta with her recently cleaned fork, with her body language saying, "I've spent so much time prodding all the bits of pasta into a neat arrangement that it seems a shame to eat it now."

"It's not a question of being afraid," I say, in a tone of voice which one hundred percent conveys amusement rather than irritation. "It's a question of playing to your strengths. Girls don't understand boys, so they try to adjust them. Boys don't understand girls, but they just accept the fact and get on with it."

Emma and Tanya do the comical jaw-drop eye-widening bit. "I got a fork here, you know," says Tanya through another mouthful of pie. "One strike to the windpipe and it's over, mate."

"You're proving my point," I say. "Girls can't follow logic, they have to drag their emotions into it."

"My emotions will punch your lights out in a minute," says Tanya, her hair tied back in pink sparkly elastic. You wouldn't think a girly girl like her would use that kind of verbal violence, would you?

Emma elegantly bites a curl of pasta and gives me a sideways smile. "All you've proved is that you boys are very bad at recognizing the truth."

I let out an exaggerated sigh and nudge Tim. "Come on, back me up here."

Tim swiftly slides his glasses back up to the bridge of his nose and gulps down a slug of the yellowy liquid that purports to be fruit juice around here. "Ummmm, well, personally I'll agree with whatever Tanya says, because she's got me quite afraid of her fork." Tanya wrinkles her nose at him appreciatively and he blushes.

"OOO!" says Tanya suddenly.

"You sat on your fork or something?" I say.

"I just remembered, must tell you," she says, "the numerology thing. Update."

"Oh yes?" says Tim, eyebrows appearing over the top of his glasses.

"Oh no," I groan.

"What's this?" says Emma.

"Plastic talk," I tell her. She nods and mouths an "oh."

"It works with more than first names," says Tanya. "Sean Appleby, eleven letters. Kurt Bartrom, eleven letters. Mike Parkins . . . Eleven . . . Letters."

"Lisa Voyd, eight letters," says Emma.

"Exactly," I say. "Doesn't work. And you've still got the Mike or Michael problem."

"It's a seventy-five-percent correlation," says Tim. "That's statistically significant."

"Thank you, Tim," says Tanya.

"Just goes to show that Lisa Voyd stands out in yet another way," I sigh.

"Give it a rest," says Emma. "I bet she's really boring in real life."

"Rubbish," I blurt. "If I'm any judge of character, she's as intensely lovely in person as she is onscreen. Probably saves lost puppy dogs or something."

"Now who's being emotional?" says Emma quietly.

"Jealous," I whisper.

"Plus!" cries Tanya. "Number of tracks on first album, twelve. Number of tracks on second album, twelve. Date of release of last single, the twelfth. Sean Appleby, age twenty-four, two times twelve . . ."

"That's totally random," I say. "That's not connected."

"It's all twelves," says Tanya.

"On the basis of that, so's your IQ," I say.

"I've still got this fork," mumbles Tanya.

Tim says he can't manage the rest of his pie and offers it to Tanya. She scrapes it onto her plate eagerly. Emma finishes her tomato-pasta-thing and spends the remainder of the lunch break organizing the notes in her not-even-slightly-battered-at-the-corners science folder.

On the way home that day, Tim says something which doesn't strike me as important at the time, but which later comes to dominate my thoughts. He's giving me a rundown on the technical problems he's been having with his FTP client software and the subsequent delays in uploading amendments to the Plastic Web site. His supermarket bag swings at his side, and I'm wondering whether it's worth pointing out to him that he's wearing odd socks. Then he does one of the radical changes of subject which characterize his conversations whenever he wants to get information out of me.

"There's a girl I like at school," he says.

"Whoa there!" I splutter. "I hope you're not being girly and emotional!"

"I—I—I'm serious, Dom. Really."

"Really?"

"Really."

"Bloody hell. Who is it?"

I'm getting slightly worried, because I genuinely don't know who he means. Dominic "Sherlock" Smith appears to be slipping up here.

"I don't want to say," he says. "You'll laugh."

"I won't," I say. I'm trying to be sensitive. Not girly! Sensitive. Not the same thing at all.

"Yes you will. I know you. All I want is something to say to her."

"What, you mean a chat-up line?"

"Nooo." He winces. "Nothing like that. It's just, you know, I'm the cerebral type . . ."

"Intellectual . . ."

"Yeh. You're more into everyday things than me, so . . ."

We do a sharp left turn in silence. We wait for a gap in the traffic (why DOES traffic bunch like that? You'd think cars were wildebeest herding across the plains), then we hop across the road in bounds like astronauts on the moon. Crossing the road at this exact point on the walk home is mandatory—twenty meters further along on our original trajectory is a florist's shop. Any closer and Tim would be sneezing till the end of next week. Florists are Tim's equivalent of garlic to a vampire. The conversation continues once we're out of nose range of stray pollen.

"Just tell her," I say. "Ask her out on a date."

"I don't like to."

"OK, don't ask her out on a date. Stay at home and pine."

"You're not being very helpful, Dom."

"You're not giving me much to work with, are you? Come on, who is it?"

"Nooo." He gives a sloping shrug, which combined with the

lollopy way he walks makes him look like he's doing a Quasimodo impression. I get the feeling he's wishing he'd never brought the subject up.

"Is it Sarah in Eleven B?"

"No."

"Is it her with the legs in Eleven B, whassername?"

"No. I'm not telling you."

Flash of inspiration. "Is it Emma?"

"No." But there's something about this particular "no" that says I'm getting closer to the truth.

"It's Tanya, isn't it?"

"Nooo!"

Bingo. "Crikey, she's twice your height, mate. Getting a snog would be like mountain climbing!"

"Shut up!"

We walk in silence for a minute or two. Tim's face suddenly looks like it's come loose from the inside, and I get a pang of remorse over having teased him.

"I reckon Emma's more your type anyway," I say.

He whips a befuddled expression at me. "You reckon?"

"Definitely. I mean, Tanya's a nice girl. Very girly girl. And of course there's the whole Plastic thing, which is important. It's vital to have stuff in common, so they say. But Emma's more your sort."

"D'you really think so? It . . . it never occurred to me before."

"Definitely. She's the cerebral type too. Little bit academic, little bit posh, little bit more your height. Perfect for you."

68

"Are you sure?" says Tim, clutching his supermarket bag all the tighter.

"Definitely."

"I'm still much more keen on Tanya," he says sadly.

I try to be tactful and consoling. "Awww, forget Tanya on that score. You're her little Plastic pal, aren't you? She doesn't think of you in that way. Besides, you could actually benefit from Emma's molding, as opposed to me. No offense."

"None taken."

"She could do wonders for your wardrobe."

I'm not sure any of that came out right. Still, the seed is sown, and my matchmaking skills are the nutrient in which it will grow.

"But . . . ," says Tim.

"But what?"

"Well . . . I always thought that the reason Emma doesn't have a boyfriend already is that . . . She's dead keen on YOU."

Eventually, after I've stopped laughing and dabbed the tears from my eyes, I express a certain surprise at Tim's suggestion.

"WHAT on EARTH makes you think THAT?"

"Well," says Tim. "I thought everyone sort of . . . Well, it's common knowledge that she—"

"Listen, Tim, the reason she's not got a boyfriend already is that she's borderline dull. She's no Lisa Voyd, is she? You know perfectly well that Lisa is my ideal woman. Emma doesn't LOOK like Lisa, she doesn't SOUND like Lisa. She's got opinions that verge on the hysterical, and so many ISSUES you'd think she was a magazine rack."

I don't really mean that. All I really mean is that . . . Actually, I don't know what I mean. I think I'm still reeling from the idea that the whole world and its dog assumes Emma's in love with me or something.

"So she's dull, hysterical and has issues," says Tim. "And she's perfect for me."

"Right."

Tim's brows twitch into a hesitant series of frowns. We say nothing else except the standard "see ya"s when we get to the corner shop, where we split directions. For the rest of the way home, I worry that I've hurt his feelings. Honesty can be a blunt instrument, after all.

But my advice must strike a chord, because in a matter of days Tim and Emma go to the cinema together. And Tim does the whole date-asking bit by himself, without once having me vet what to say. Makes me almost proud of him, it does. They go to see some dreadful chick flick about a woman with a disease or a dead cat or something.

"Was it brain-guttingly awful?" I say.

"No, it was really good," says Tim.

"You see, you're made for each other."

He is forced to agree.

Tanya goes through a few days of giving Tim soulful little looks, and I begin to wonder if I've miscalculated her attitude towards him, but then things settle down and I wonder no longer.

Tim and Emma don't exactly become an item, though. All they seem to do is make the odd trip to the latest arthouse indie movie critical smash. Still, it keeps Tim in an optimistic frame of mind, and it gives Emma a more worthwhile project to work on, so I'm not complaining. All's right with the world.

It's about nine o'clock the following Sunday evening. I'm flopped on my bed reading through a stack of posts from Plastic fans printed out via Tim's Web site. Some of these people have very interesting things to say. Some of them are total loonies.

There's a soft almost-knock at my door. Being engrossed in my work, I barely register it, but then it almost-sounds again and I look up. "Hello?"

Long pause. There it is again, like a small rodent trying to get out of a box. I go over and open the door. Dad's standing there, knuckles raised ready to knock again.

"Oh. Hi, Dom! I don't want to disturb you, I didn't know if you . . . were asleep or anything."

". . . No."

"Can I come in?"

I aim a finger like a revolver at the chair beside my desk. Dad gives me a soppy grin and a nod and flops into the chair. There's a silence that couldn't be more uncomfortable if it were filled with boiling lava.

"So, how you doing, Dom?"

"Fine. Why?"

"Oooh, no reason. We just, you know, haven't had a good chat recently. I wouldn't want you to think you couldn't discuss things with me."

"There's nothing I want to say, Dad."

"Because you can say, if you need to. Whenever."

"Whenever you're around, sure."

Dad sniffs and shuffles, and starts leafing through the sheets of paper on my desk. "Dom, you mustn't think that you can't come to me if you need to talk. You and Seb. I mean, don't think you can't e-mail me at the office, even."

"We know we can, Dad."

Dad's eyes track around the posters and charts and notes pinned to my walls, moving in slow circles which you'd think would make him go dizzy. He quietly clacks his teeth together a few times.

"Obviously Mum and I have demanding jobs, which means we can't always . . . It's that, you know, we want to give you boys the things in life that others, like Mum, might not have had growing up. You know, growing up with Gran and Grandad."

"Yes, Dad."

"The thing is, just because your mother is always out of the house, doesn't mean . . . Well, it would have been nice for her to talk to you with me, like we'd arranged. She must have got delayed at work or something. Look, you don't have to wait for her to come home, you can bring problems to me."

"Yes, Dad."

"Are there . . . any problems bothering you at the moment?"

"No, Dad."

"Sure? Phew, I'm glad I'm not a teenager these days, eh?"

"There is nothing bothering me. I promise."

"You know, girl trouble, police warnings . . ."

"Daaaad!"

"Right. Good. Fine. Glad to hear it." He nods slowly, sagely. "You're a sensible boy. You're both sensible boys. We trust you."

He turns over a couple of the Plastic CDs on my desk. "I don't think I've heard these, have I?"

"You probably have, Dad."

"By 'eck, she's a good-looking lass. Crikey, if I was thirty years younger, eh? Ha ha . . . Sorry. What are you reading?"

"It's posts from Tim's Web site, mostly about the itinerary for Plastic's tour of Europe next month."

"Oh. Right." I can see he's thinking of adding some advice about how travel broadens the mind, but eventually he decides against it. He stands and gives me a swift clap on the shoulder. "Well, I'm glad we had a talk, Dom." Then he goes downstairs to catch *Enterprise* on Channel Four.

"I'm me today, I'm you tomorrow
A face for a face to beg or borrow"

—"Me Me Me," from the Plastic album *Highly Offensive*
(Voyd/Parkins © Cellophane Music Ltd)

1:29 p.m. Lift time elapsed: sixty-two minutes.

Through the glass sides of the lift, I can see that Tim is still gazing up at me. He straightens his glasses and I see him sneeze a couple of times into the back of his hand. His lungs must be playing up in the heat and smell of the crowd. Behind me, Lisa is rhythmically clunking her phone against the floor.

Tanya is talking animatedly to the fan in the bright green pullover, and whoever else is within earshot of her. She is making flat, un-equivocal hand gestures and, here and there, subtly pointing towards me. Faces keep flipping between her and me, all of them filled with the same jealous-joy clash that Tim and Tanya showed when the lift first stopped.

The fan in the green pullover switches batteries on his video camera and takes several long, lingering shots of me. I sit motionless. For some reason I can't even explain to myself, I suddenly want his footage to be as uninteresting as possible.

The balding shop manager with the ID badge is still keeping a hand hovering around the clipped-and-cased phone at his waist. Remember I said about Manky Milo at school, about how I knew it was him who was nicking computer lab stuff? This manager reminds me of that little incident. He's got that same air about him of doing something he shouldn't, right under everyone's noses. I watch him check that a door tucked away behind the sales desk is locked, in a way which is far too deliberately casual.

The Big Deal Records staff are doing swift business behind that sales desk. The knot of ten-year-old girls in Plastic sweatshirts are now clutching Big Deal carriers to their chests, yattering together and being moved along past the wire rack of shrinkwrapped T-shirts by the guards. The news crews seem to be waiting impatiently.

Tim gives me the thumbs-up, which is clearly the only way he can think of to communicate with me. He smiles broadly between coughs. I can hear his voice, and Tanya's, in my head, breathless, happy: "What's she like? What did she say? What did you say to her?"

What do I tell them? Suddenly there's a gap between me and them which has nothing to do with glass or the height of the lift.

"Bob?" barks Lisa. I turn to see her huddled in her corner, head down, phone to her ear. "Yes, I know what you said! But I want to know what's going on! . . . Well, WHEN, for Christ's sake? . . . I'm perfectly relaxed, thank you! . . . No! No, NOW!"

She hands me the phone again with a you-talk-to-him finality.

". . . to be patient, dear. You haven't been in there too long, so don't start whining. If that rat turd in there with you is getting on your nerves you'll have to—"

"Hello, Mr. Fullbright. Me again."

"Get off that phone!"

I hand it back.

Without switching it off, she bashes the phone to the floor and smashes it apart with the heel of her boot in half a dozen vertical kicks. She runs her hands through her hair, letting out an exasperated growl.

I glance back down in time to see the tall, wiry figure of Bob Fullbright crossing the shop in the direction of the sales desk. He must have been standing close to the lift shaft until now. He's wearing a patterned jacket and red shoes, in the manner of someone with no imagination who thinks they're a lovable eccentric. His hair is so gelled it looks more like feathers. He makes a beeline for the shop manager. They exchange a few words, then Mr. Baldy pulls the phone from his waistband and retreats into a corner. He whips a slip of paper from his pocket and quickly taps out the number that must be written on it.

"Do you trust your manager?"

"What?" says Lisa. I'm keeping my eye on Mr. Baldy.

"Do you trust Bob Fullbright?"

"He's a slimy little weasel who'd sell his granny to Satan if it'd get him into the papers. Can't stand him. Why?"

"No reason."

* * *

It's late November, one week ago. One week before "Meet Lisa Voyd! Signing Copies of Plastic's New Album! At the Grand Opening of Big Deal Records, Birmingham's Latest, Greatest Entertainment Retailer!" It's the night of the school concert, which is three weeks early this year because the main hall's being refurbished for the remainder of the term.

The concert always packs as many pupils as possible into the actual onstage stuff. This is so that, says the headmaster, participation in a creative and confidence-building event is available to all year groups. The real reason, says the rest of us, is so that the maximum number of mums, dads, aunties, uncles, cousins, little sisters and household pets are obliged to attend. Ticket sales boost the school budget.

This year, there's the usual mix of the sublime and the ridiculous. The A-level English set are doing the last scene from an Arthur Miller play; the whole of 7B are reciting self-penned limericks; Veronica "Spex" Thomas is singing Victorian music hall songs accompanied by Emma on the piaaaano; Miniature Dwight is doing his magic act (again!); and so on and so forth, blah blah blah, tea and biscuits to be served in the interval.

And then, of course, there's me, Tim, Tanya, Bruce from 11A and Silent Dave from 9G. We're the "sublime" part of the mix, third act on after the tea and biscuits. We are Plastic Bag, tribute band extraordinaire. The name was inspired by Tim's supermarket carrier.

Tim IS Sean Appleby on keyboard, Bruce from 11A IS Kurt Bartrom on drums, Silent Dave IS Mike Parkins on guitar. We've included Bruce because they didn't need him in 11A's tableau of the twentieth century, and he would have missed out otherwise. We've included Silent Dave because he's the only person we could find who could play the guitar and was willing to do it. Tim can't actually play the keyboard—all the sounds are preprogrammed, he just moves his fingers about and mimes.

Tanya's role is to represent the screaming masses. She leaps around the stage dressed in hat and coat like a stereotype 1950s journalist, wielding a chunky camera and taking flash photos of the band. It's a TOTALLY naff concept, I know, but it was the only way to get Plastic Bag past the headmaster. She normally vetoes suggestions which involve pop music, but we managed to convince her that the addition of Tanya gives the whole thing an arty edge which makes a comment on modern society and the media. Yeh, right.

But wait, you say, who IS Lisa Voyd?

Me! Tanya didn't want to be Lisa for the simple reason that she can't sing a note, and so didn't want to damage the reputation of the foremost singer-songwriter of our generation. The good news is that Tanya, being the strapping but girly lass she is, has plenty of sparkly clothes which fit me perfectly.

On the morning when the checklist of acts and available rehearsal times goes up on the notice board, Emma asks me what exactly "Plastic Bag: Smith, 10N, *et al*" entails. When I tell her she's so shocked she leaves a speck of fluff unattended on her blazer for almost five minutes.

"You are kidding," she says, eyes flitting back and forth between me and Tanya. "Tell me you're kidding."

"What's your problem?" I protest. "We've started rehearsing already. In Tanya's garage."

"With you as female lead singer?"

"Yes," I say. "It's IRONIC. Plastic's lyrics are steeped in irony and meaning, subverting the conventions of popular music in wordplay and logical twists of the unexpected."

"So you're dressing up as the female lead singer," says Emma.

"It's not *dressing up!*" I cry. "It's a tribute band! It's IRONIC!"

"Dom, there are some guys in this school who'd look, y'know, amusing in a dress. Some guys could make it really funny. But . . . Dominic . . . You're not one of them. And you can't sing."

"I sing better than Tanya."

"No, you don't! You sound like a strangled cat!"

She keeps on protesting right up until the big night itself, in a tone which gets ever more high-pitched as the days progress. She gets particularly stroppy one evening when she happens to call at Tanya's and sees the full force of my seriously authentic Voyd strutting and my falsetto vocals.

"Oh, Dominic, you look stupid and you sound even worse!"

It occurs to me that she's simply worried we'll blow her performance out of the water. Emma and Spex are the last act of the evening but, frankly, once they've witnessed Plastic Bag, who are the mums, dads, aunties, uncles, cousins, little sisters and household pets going to be talking about on the way home? Eh?

It's the night of the concert. With the cast numbering several dozen, the small backstage area of the main hall is already overflowing with Year Sevens and Eights. Plastic Bag, along with Emma and one or two other acts, are getting ready in the sports equipment area that joins the foyer of the hall. To be more specific, Plastic Bag are allocated the walk-in cupboard where they keep the hurdles and footballs. Emma's been entrusted with the keys to everything, on pain of death should she lose them.

Tim is in costume, perched on the summit of the vaulting horse. "It's got me thinking, all of this," he says, continuously flipping the CD-ROM with all his keyboard's MIDI data on it. "I could have a real shot at being in the actual Plastic."

Bruce from 11A emits a spluttery laugh as he ties his shoelaces. Silent Dave says nothing. He's peering at his spots in the handheld mirror that's our only means of checking our appearance.

"Don't you think?" says Tim.

"Tim," I say. "You can't actually play that keyboard."

"Yeh, but it's just a skill you can learn, isn't it? I mean, it's more important to be someone who'll fit into the band, right?"

"Tim, I think if they were looking for someone they'd look for an actual keyboard PLAYER first, wouldn't they?"

"But if they WERE looking for someone, surely it'd make sense to hire a devoted fan like you or me? Someone who knows what Plastic's all about, who can fit into the harmony of their lives?"

My face crumples and twists for a moment. "But . . . they're NOT looking for someone, are they! And they're hardly likely to."

"Ah!" says Tim. The CD-ROM stops flipping and he holds up a finger as if it'll make us all pay attention. "Sean Appleby's not the fittest person in the world, is he? Remember, they had to cancel the Paris concert because he had a chest infection."

He sniffs back a fresh glob of snot. I can't help thinking that this peculiar little outburst is down to Emma's molding influence, all her talk of achievements and "making the effort."

"So," I say at last, "when Mrs. Thingummy drags you into the Careers Office and asks you what you want to do when you've left school, you're going to tell her you're pinning your hopes on Sean Appleby of Plastic dropping dead and you being on the top of Bob Fullbright's short list of replacements?"

"I'm not saying it's going to happen," says Tim quietly. "I'm just saying, you know, IF . . ."

"I think this concert's going to your head," I say. I fling my arms out and rotate, like I'm on a slow turntable. "OK, people, tell me how totally FANTASTIC I am!"

I've got the wig, I've got the padded bra, I've got the boots, I've got the lot. The four of us look each other up and down, grinning broadly.

"That is seriously weird, Smith," says Bruce of 11A, smirking. "When the whole school out there sees and hears YOU . . . Ooooh boy, I can't wait for the reaction." He smirks some more, darkly.

Silent Dave's upper lip curls with uncertainty. Tim clambers down from the vaulting horse. They look thoroughly authentic—right clothes, right attitude, right everything. Silent Dave's even got the same shaped nose as Mike Parkins (slightly lumpy at the end).

"C'mon, guys, this is no time for nerves," I say. "As to the reaction? They'll be stunned! Right! Time?"

"Twenty minutes," says Tim.

We form a huddle.

"OK, this is it," I whisper. "We are gonna damn well ROCK!"

In perfect unison, the four of us give a loud warrior yell, fists clenched, arms tensed in bodybuilder pose.

The noise brings the girls clop-clopping from their dressing room, behind the stack of rubber floor mats. Tanya appears around the open door of our cupboard and shrieks at me. "Dom! Wow!"

"How the hell do you walk in these heels?" I cry.

"Don't you stretch them!"

She's ready with coat, hat and camera. Spex Thomas and Emma are right behind her, in long formal black dresses. Spex kind of spasms when she sees me, takes a quick rub at her pebble-thick lenses, then spasms all over again. "Oh my God," she mumbles. Then Emma gets a look at me. She turns so pale she's practically transparent.

You see? They're seething with indignation that Plastic Bag will be the big hit of the evening.

Spex is fluttering like a butterfly in a jam jar. "Emma, where's the sheet music? Oh, it's in the hall, isn't it. Do I look all right? Be honest. Have you got those keys?"

"You're fine," says Emma. "We're both fine. I've got everything."

"You're hideous," chortles Bruce from 11A from behind a cupped hand.

"Shut up!" squeaks Spex. "Don't say that!"

"Come on, then, everyone," cries Tanya. Everyone starts to make their way out into the hall foyer. Everyone except Emma. She gently holds a hand against my chest, telling me to stay put.

"You lot go ahead!" she calls. "I just need a word with Dominic."

Bruce from 11A cups his hand again. "Snog!"

"I guess you're dying to tell me how gorgeous I look," I say.

Emma's face displays what can only be called an un-smile. "Dominic, PLEASE, it's not too late. Let Tanya do it. You take the photos."

"Don't be silly, she can't sing. What's this about?"

"YOU can't sing. Dom, please, I'm begging you, don't do this. Even Bruce from Eleven A could make it funny. Even Tim could make it funny. You take it too seriously. You don't look funny at all. You look creepy."

I stare into her eyes for a moment, puzzled. They're huge and blue, sharp as a pin; it's the rest of her that gives an impression of crying.

"It's not meant to get laughs, it's a tribute act!" I say. "This is jealousy, isn't it? This is because it's something I'm beating you on, hands down."

"NO!" she shouts. The sound reverberates in the foyer. A few muffled voices can be heard out there. Her hand grips the front of my blouse and she speaks softly, almost in a whisper. "I don't want you making a total fool of yourself. It's toe-curling enough without the dress, but WITH it . . ."

"The dress is half the point! It's IRONIC! You've got no sense of humor, that's your trouble."

She tweaks at my skirt. "There's no humor involved! Will you PLEASE trust me on this? You've got it wrong, this once, OK? I understand why you think it's great, I really do, but I promise you—I PROMISE you—if you go out there and turn yourself into a prancing embarrassment, you'll regret it more than anything in your whole life."

"I'll be famous."

"You'll be in a lot of trouble."

"But I'll still be famous."

"You'll be the village idiot! LISTEN TO ME! That's our school out there, not an audience of Plastic fans! They don't care how *ironic* it is!"

"They'll all be talking about me tomorrow."

"Of course they will, you'll have ruined the whole concert!"

I take a step back. "I was right. It's just sour grapes, isn't it. Bloody sour grapes."

With a strangulated cry, she pushes me hard and I tumble off my heels. Before I scramble upright, she's slammed the door and kla-klicked the key in the lock. I bang violently with both palms until they sting.

"EMMA! LET ME OUT!"

There's a slow scraping sound on the other side of the door. Only later do I realize she must be sliding down it to the floor.

"Let me OUT! You miserable . . . I'll never forgive you for this, do you hear me? LET ME OUT!"

After a quick backstage costume makeover, which basically amounts to ditching the coat, hat and camera, Tanya goes on in my place. Plastic Bag are not a riotous success. Once the whole thing's finished, Tim finds the keys taped to the door and he lets me out. Emma is long gone.

I change and walk out to the car park at the front of the school. Grandad drives us home, with Gran and Seb in the back of the car and me propped against the passenger seat window, staring out at the passing streetlights.

"You were very convincing," says Gran. "You looked just like a girl."

"Gave me the shudders," mumbled Grandad.

In my pale reflection in the window, here then gone again as we pass the streetlights, I notice that I've forgotten to remove the eye shadow.

"Sour grapes, huh?" says Lisa.

(1:38 p.m. Lift time elapsed: seventy-one minutes.)

"Yeh. I was furious!"

"You were furious. Standing there in your wig and your padded bra, you were furious, were you?" says Lisa. She's eyeing me with her head tilted forward.

"It was IRONIC!"

"No, it was STUPID! Our album titles, they're ironic. Some of my lyrics, they're ironic, the way we did the video for 'Happy Clappy,' that's ironic. I'm with Emma on this one. There's a fine line, right, between doing-what-you-did-and-making-it-funny, and doing-what-you-did-and-looking-like-a-sad-fanboy-in-drag, and she could tell that YOU were on the wrong side of that line! GOT IT?"

There go those icebergs again, drifting apart: one, my thoughts on Lisa up until today; the other, my thoughts about her now. Several different sentences form themselves in my head, but not one of them makes it to my mouth. All that emerges is a weak "I thought you'd be flattered."

"Well, you thought wrong. You seem to think a lot of things wrong, don't you. Eh, Dominic?" She zips out a hand to shut me up. "And don't start dribbling out some pathetic explanation. I don't want to know WHY."

"Look, I never meant to—"

"Have you heard of oxytocin?"

Huh? I think carefully for a minute. ". . . No."

"It's what you'd call the 'maternal' hormone. Teenagers are awash with it. It's one of the things that accounts for crazies like you, and crowds like them down there in the shop. It's what makes boys tend to identify with their heroes, and girls worship them. You really think things like that aren't taken into account when it comes to people like Bob selling people like me to people like you? You're all slaves to growing up. You're all little clockwork consumers. Stick that in your chemistry homework."

There's a long silence. "Is that true?"

"I read a lot," says Lisa. "Trust me. Like you should trust Emma."

"She locked me in a cupboard last week!"

"SHE THINKS THE WORLD OF YOU!" Lisa's almost on her hands and knees, the force of her voice almost pulling her towards me. "And if you had a single molecule of sense, you'd admit you think the world of her too!"

"She keeps trying to mold me!"

"She keeps trying to kick you out of the cave you live in! Everything she says to you is exactly what I'D say to you! You fill your life with trivia and distractions, and it breaks her heart!"

"She locked me in a closet!"

"She'd rather have had you hate her than let you make a prat of yourself! CAN'T YOU SEE THAT?" Lisa is all but screaming at me now. "She's sick of the rubbish you fill your head with!"

"It's not rubbish! I think more of you and Plastic than I do of her!"

"You don't know me! You don't know any of us! It's all flashing lights and My Favorite Ice Cream!"

"Oh, so if I was into Bach and Beethoven that'd be OK, would it?"

"No, not if you buried your head in it, no! Does Emma bury her head in her music? Does she? No! I bet there's a dozen other things going on in her life, worthwhile things, real things, but you don't acknowledge all that, do you? You don't see it. All you try to see in her is what doesn't fit your own TINY, TINY, LITTLE WORLD!"

"ENOUGH!" I yell. "Shut up, I've had ENOUGH!"

I can't look at her. My arms are around my head, as if to keep it from exploding. This is Lisa Voyd! Lisa Voyd! Lisa Voyd, who I love and admire, Lisa Voyd, the famous, the stylish, the shining, the talented. I always thought . . . I was so sure she'd . . . Lisa Voyd, I'm nothing to her. She's nothing to me. I can't keep track of it anymore.

There go those melting icebergs. Drifting ever further apart.

Breathing hard, I look down, through the glass. There, beside Tim and Tanya.

It's Emma. She's unmistakable with that hair. She hugs them both.

I have a twisting sensation in my chest.

1:44 p.m.

"My love is like a red, red nose
It runs all through the wintertime"

—"News of the Girl," from the Plastic album *From Hell It Came*
(Voyd/Parkins © Cellophane Music Ltd)

Lift time elapsed: seventy-seven minutes.

I hate Christmas. Bah, humbug. There's something fake and compulsory about the whole thing which makes me want to hide under the bedcovers and not come out until it's well and truly Next Year.

I don't mind the presents, of course. That bit's OK. And when the tree's sitting there in the corner of the darkened living room, twinkling away to itself, I suppose the tiniest microbe of Yuletide cheer manages to snuggle down in my lap. But that's it. That's really it. I absolutely loathe all the tatty decorations and the bad-tempered shopping and the enforced jollity of the Big Day.

My family spends the entire Christmas period assuming that a Fixed Smile Act has just been made law. If it ever was, we'd all be slung in prison by Boxing Day. What makes the entire event all the worse is the weather. On cards, on TV, on festive biscuit tins it's all snow, snow, snow, snowmen, ho ho ho, sleigh rides, jingly bells and snow. Outside, it's pouring rain. Every Christmas is a festival of sob-bing gray skies and damp winds. I swear the whole meteorological system of Northern Europe is just taking the mickey for the sake of it.

Last Christmas, eleven months ago, is a case in point. Quite mild and pleasant right up to the middle of December, and then zap: we're living on the frozen tundra of the West Midlands. Not a sin-gle snowflake, naturally, just searing cold that stings your face and makes you lose all communication with your feet.

Christmas Day dawns in the Smith residence as it has dawned for these many years past, with the cry of the wild Sebastian calling the family to gather at the foot of the tree and dish out the pressies.

"For God's sake, Seb," comes the muffled cry of Dad from under his pillow. "It's five in the morning!"

Twenty minutes later, we're assembled in the living room. I'm huddled in an armchair in my dressing gown, trying to wake up. Gran is clattering about in the kitchen, sounding out the Clanking of the Saucepans which heralds the traditional Getting Ready of the Brussels Sprouts. Grandad is sitting forward in his chair, fingers deli-cately poised on forehead, patiently waiting for someone to ask him if he feels all right. Mum and Dad are kneeling either side of the tree, glowing with pride as their youngest son rips cheerfully through sheet after sheet of snow-patterned wrapping paper. Everyone's hair looks like their brains just exploded.

Seb's evil-little-brat persona has been temporarily replaced with the wide-eyed-happy-child one he saves for birthdays and Christmas. "Awww, thaaaanks Mum! Thanks Dad!" "WoooooWWWWW! This is

EXACTLY what I wanted!" "Waaaaahhhh! Awesome! Billy Clench at school has got this one!"

I manage to retain my dignity with a performance that's low on gushing sentiment, while retaining a suitable level of genuine pleasure and gratitude. Mum and Dad seem to prefer the Seb approach.

"Look at the state of me," announces Mum. "I'm going to get washed and dressed." As Seb sets his new Action Man Anti-Terrorist Unit to take out all evildoers with maximum bloodshed, Mum stands and cocks her head sideways at Grandad. For the merest, tiniest snip of time you can see her resist the urge to say what's required of her, but she buckles under pressure in the end. "You all right, there, Grandad?"

Three-second pause. "Yeh. I'm fine, love. Touch of me neck trouble, that's all."

Mum moves on. Gran marches in from the kitchen. She's already dressed and heavily made up. "Will one saucepan of sprouts be enough for everyone?"

Several hours later I'm sitting on the stairs and I call Emma. She loves Christmas. Adores it.

"Happy Christmaaaaas!" she squeals down the phone.

I smile and give a small shake of the head. "Hiya."

"I'm wearing my party hat!"

"I don't doubt it."

"It's in a cone shape," she says enticingly, as if that's going to change my mind about party hats. "With silver stripes. Are you wearing your party hat, Dom? No no, don't tell me, let me guess,

ummmmmmm, oooh, I'm getting a psychic vibe here, I see . . . I
see . . . no hat whatsoever!"

"Correct!"

"Woo-hoo, I'm right again, Party Pooper!"

"I am not a party pooper."

She blows a loud raspberry and I hold my phone at arm's length
for a second. "Anyway," I say, eventually, "I'm just calling to say hi
and that I've got you a Christmas pressie here."

"For meeeee?" she pipes in a girly voice. "Awww, Dommy, you
wittew sweetie!"

"Have you been at your mum's sherry?"

"Oh, come on, Scrooge, it's Christmas!"

"Only, I've not had a chance to see you since school finished, otherwise I'd have brought it round yesterday. Can I pop round later?
I'm desperate to get out of the house for a bit."

"Sorry, PooperMan, but we're having to get out of the house ourselves."

"Oh, are you all going to see your sister?"

"No, she's at some country place with her friends for the day,
lucky moo. We've been ordered out 'cos there's a gas leak in the
street."

"Gas leak?" I say.

"Gas leak?" says Mum, inching past me on her way upstairs.

"At Emma's," I say hurriedly. "Not here. I can't smell gas, don't panic."

Mum stops passing and stays put, her fluffy slippers level with
my head.

"British Gas rang the bell a minute ago," says Emma. "Apparently it's the freezing weather—there's a main pipe burst or something. They'll be all day fixing it and everyone in the street is having to clear out for safety."

"Bummer. Where are you going to go?"

"Dad doesn't want to drive all the way to my uncle Matt's because of all the ice, so he says we might see if there are places left at that big hotel by the M40."

"Fun," I say. "I bet you'll have to beat half your neighbors to it!"

Mum plucks the phone from my fingers. "Hallo? Emma? It's Dominic's mum, have I got that right, are you having to . . . ? Really? . . . Oh, no, and on Christmas Day! . . . Is it? . . . Yes, I'm sure they are . . . Well, come over here for the day, the three of you!"

Oh God, no!

". . . Yeees, of course! . . . No, the more the merrier, we'd love to have you, and you won't be too far from home so you can keep an eye on how the workmen are . . . Yes! Put your mum on the phone."

Oh God in heaven. Not at MY house, not with MY family! I thought there were STRICT CONVENTIONS about not fraternizing with the Lawrences? I thought there was supposed to be a perfectly clear and unbreachable social RULE?

A few minutes later, Mum switches the phone off and finally stops playing about with her hair. She darts looks into every corner of the hall, like a sparrow on full alert.

"Muuum," I say weakly, "but you've never in your life invited Emma's family over!"

"Oh, for goodness' sake, Dominic, it's Christmas! Get the hoover! They'll be here in twenty minutes. Gran! Get more sprouts ready!"

I'm ordered to hoover the hall and living room. Dad is sent to clean the bathroom and make-sure-you-do-the-toilet-properly-I-know-what-you're-like. Seb is dragged away from defusing an atomic device that's about to flatten the Coventry area and forced to make the beds and check all areas for stray mugs. Dad finishes the bathroom and is sent to change his shirt. I finish the hoovering and am handed a duster and a can of spray polish.

"They're not flippin' royalty!" I protest.

"They're guests," says Mum, "and I will not have this house looking like a rubbish tip."

Typical, I think to myself, as I wipe the top of the telly. She's perfectly happy for US to live with the dust, but when it's EMMA's lot coming over, oooh NOOO, suddenly we live in a tip.

Mum collars me on her way up to switch dresses for the second time. She leans over to me conspiratorially. "Put a bit of air freshener on Grandad's chair," she whispers.

Can of Nice 'n' Fresh in hand, I slope into the living room. Grandad is examining the brightly colored box containing Seb's hugely exciting new board game, an overpriced collection of plastic pieces entitled Pig in a Barrel. Slowly and dolefully, he reads the bouncy lettering under the title: *"It's . . . a barrel . . . of family fun . . ."*

I pull him forward and direct a huge hissing spray all over the back of the armchair. "Sorry, Grandad, orders is orders."

DDrrrrrrrring.

From the way they react, you'd think the bell had sent half a million volts through my parents. Dad shoots to the front door. I've tucked myself away in the kitchen, millimeters out of range of Gran's swooshing saucepans. From the hall comes a burble of voices, hellos and nice-to-see-you's. A few seconds later Mum bustles into the kitchen carrying a cardboard six-pack of red wine bottles and an elongated pot of paté.

"Look what the Lawrences brought for us, isn't that nice?" she says, as if they were standing at her shoulder and I was hard of thinking. "Go on in, Dominic," she whispers. "Talk to them while I put these in the fridge."

Emma looks immaculate as usual, in a gray-blue ensemble. Somehow the pointy party hat suits her. Her parents don't have her fashion perfectionism, but the briefest glance is enough to tell you that the Smiths and the Lawrences are unlikely to bump into each other while out clothes shopping. The jacket her dad is sporting must be one he wears to work, because the cap of a cheap ballpoint is poking out of his top pocket. He's every bit as tall as Emma isn't, with a hawkish nose, and hands and feet which seem slightly too big for the rest of him. Mrs. Lawrence is all smiles and spectacles. If you drew her, you wouldn't use a single straight line anywhere.

Mr. Lawrence lifts off the sofa slightly to shake me by the hand. A formal gesture like that always makes me feel uneasy, and I'm pretty sure he realizes that.

"Haven't seen you in ages, young man," he says in his chocolate-box tones. "Always hearing about you, though." He raises a bushy eyebrow at Emma, in a way that's obviously calculated to get her saying "Daaaad." But she's too busy gazing happily at the Christmas tree to notice.

Dad looks like he wants to respond in a similar vein but, since I never talk to him about Emma much, he can't. There is an awkward silence.

"Who's going to play Pig in a Barrel with me?" pipes up Seb.

"Ooo, I will," replies Emma, sticking her hand in the air. She slides off the armchair and hands-and-knees it with Seb over to the empty space by the dining room door.

"Did you get that today?" says Emma.

"Yeh! And an Action Man Anti-Terrorist Unit!"

"Fantastic! I wish they'd done those for Barbie."

"And a pullover off me auntie Sue. We both got one."

"Never mind."

Damn, why didn't I think of that? Emma's got herself out of the awkward silence now! Damn!

"Can three play?" I call to Seb.

"No."

Back at the sofa there is another awkward silence. It's only now we've got guests in the house I remember that the coffee table in our living room is Gran and Grandad's garden one from their old house. Dark green plastic. Mr. Lawrence is looking at it. It's getting close to lunchtime.

At lunch, we all crowd into the dining room. The nine of us just about fit at the table. Dad is sent to fetch my desk chair and Seb's desk chair from upstairs, in order to close the chair gap. I get Seb's, Seb gets mine. He sits there swinging his legs and itching to pull a cracker.

"Mum," I say, as the platters of vegetables are brought in, "can't I have MY chair?"

"No," growls Mum. "Seb's is too low for him at this table."

I look at where the table touches my pullover from Auntie Sue, a fraction below chest height. My eyes are level with Emma's shoulders. She peers down at me with a hello-shorty look on her face.

"Don't," I tell her quietly. She smirks.

Mum has seated us all. Around the table: Mum (nearest the kitchen door so she can fetch things), Mrs. Lawrence, Dad, Mr. Lawrence, Emma, me, Seb, Grandad, Gran (nearest the window so she can open it for Grandad when he gets his funny tum). We all have space equivalent to the width of one white dinner plate, plus a little bit. Several of us are wider than that.

Mum has a seizure of panic when she sends Dad to bring the turkey in. "Ohgoodgrief, you're not vegetarians, are you?"

The Lawrences smile and shake their heads. "Noo, noo, that's fine," says Mr. Lawrence.

"I'm so sorry," says Mum, hand to chest, "I never even thought to ask. That's 'cos of Dad distracting me with hunting for the corkscrew."

Dad appears, big silver dish in arms, turkey steaming away to itself. The corkscrew is dangling from his little finger. "Found it, Mum," he announces. "Where I said it was."

There's a multihanded shifting of plates, wineglasses and cutlery to make space for the turkey dish on the table. "There we go," says Dad, bringing it in to land like an edible helicopter. "Whoops! Sorry! Ah, that's it. Should have used the smaller dish after all, eh, Mum?"

"Our eldest daughter's a vegetarian," says Mrs. Lawrence, to make conversation.

"Oh!" says Mum. "That's interesting." She nods. In social situations, Mum is a nodder; she's one of those people who does a twitchy couple of head movements after they've spoken, as if the sound of their voice pulls on a cord in their neck.

"Ooo, I don't hold with them veggies, me," says Gran.

"Is your daughter still in London?" says Mum at a slightly higher volume.

"She's spending Christmas with friends," says Mrs. Lawrence. "They've rented a cottage for the week."

"Oh, how lovely," says Mum, nod, nod. "I'd love to do that one year."

"It's not natural," says Gran. "I'd make all them veggies eat nothing but meat for a week, I would, see how THEY like it! Ooo, I'm a right terror, I am." She giggles and Mr. Lawrence flinches.

"Do help yourselves, everyone!" cries Mum. "We don't stand on ceremony. Ohgoodgrief, you're not religious, are you? Do you say grace?"

The Lawrences smile and shake their heads. "Nooo, no no," says Mr. Lawrence, "we're a pretty secular lot."

"Ooo, my sisters would have your guts for garters," says Gran. "They don't agree with them sects. All my family's Methodist."

"Gran!" cries Mum sweetly. "Better not get you started on religion, eh? Not on Christmas Day."

"There's lots of people you'd have shot, aren't there, Granny!" says Seb.

"I'm terrible, I am," says Gran, play-boxing with him.

There's a steady clattering of serving spoons on china. Gran's first to everything, and goes at her piled plateful like a warthog at a watering hole. I'm fairly sure she's left a load of chestnut stuffing in the oven, but there's no way I'm saying anything.

Seb's happily cramming roast potatoes into his mouth, which at least keeps him quiet. Dad starts talking to Mr. Lawrence about work. Mr. Lawrence hovers over his plate, knife and fork held like toys in those weirdly large hands, as he keeps Dad spellbound.

"I'm involved in a research project at the moment," he says. "We're studying cognitive development in the early years. Specifically the effect of environment on intelligence. It's amazing what little ones are capable of."

Mum shoots a glance at Seb. Seb's got his cheeks puffed out like a hamster.

"And how's the world of IT management?" says Mr. Lawrence.

Dad sets his fork down delicately. "Actually, we've recently ported our old Unix system over to an array of Apple G5 servers running ten-three-three."

"Oh dear, Dad, you'll have us all dropping asleep in our gravy," says Mum.

"Not at all," says Mr. Lawrence. "Computers are a bit of a hobby of mine."

Emma and her mum do a theatrical groan. Her dad swivels to face Emma, hand on hip. "You don't complain when I fix your laptop, young lady."

"Now I've reconfigured the network," continues Dad, "almost all the cross-platform issues we were having before have been ironed out. User callouts were all but eliminated last week. Ha ha, we'll be making ourselves redundant at this rate!"

"So, that was a sensible move, then," says Mum.

"It's got me a lot of praise from the boardroom," says Dad with a smile made of iron.

Grandad lifts his plate a couple of centimeters off the table and towards Mum. "I don't know if you can, like, but these sprouts need warming up, love, could you?"

Mum takes the plate and weaves her way into the kitchen soundlessly. Gran pauses slightly between chews. "Are you all right, Seednee?" she twitters, without looking in his direction. "Do you need the window open?"

Grandad considers carefully for three seconds. "No. 'M OK, love."

Dad wheels his conversational cycle around to Mrs. Lawrence. "Have you been busy with Christmas, Barbara?"

"Very," says Mrs. Lawrence. "For some reason I always seem to have a rush of patients at this time of year."

Grandad perks up like a puppy. "Patients?"

Mrs. Lawrence takes a second to realize who said that. "Err, yes, I'm a doctor."

"Are ya?" he says, perking up some more. "Are you on call today, like?"

"Umm, actually I'm not a GP, I work over at the hospital."

"I reckon I'll have to go to the hospital. I've got this shooting pain goes from me neck down me side." He runs a finger down the path of his shooting pain. "Shoots all the way down. What do you reckon it is?"

"Umm, necks aren't really my area, I'm afraid."

"Shoots all down me side, it does."

"Probably best if you go and see your GP," says Mrs. Lawrence.

Grandad droops and gives a grunt which translates as "Well, if you're going to be like that I won't bother, then." Mum comes back with Grandad's freshly microwaved plate and sets it down in front of him.

"He's useless, our doctor," chirps Gran. "I can't follow his accent. He's Hungranarian or summat, all 'c's and 'x's in his name. Mind you, they're all useless. My sister went to her doctor with her foot and it was her kidneys all along, they never spotted it till she came over all funny in the post office."

"How did we get onto this?" pipes Mum, alarmed. "Would any-body like more sprouts? There's only Grandad eaten any."

Everybody except Grandad mumbles a polite no-thank-you. Suddenly, Gran leaps to her feet. Her knife drops into her carrots with a thud.

"Ooo!" she squeaks. For a second we all stare at her. "I've left the stuffing in the oven!"

An hour later, Gran and Mum are in the kitchen fighting cheerily over the washing up. The stuffing is in the bin. Seb and Action Man are burrowing through the litter of Christmas cracker shreds and blobs of pudding on the dining room table, on their vital mission to rid the world of all anti-Yuletide scum. Dad is trying to demonstrate the features of our DTV set-top box using the remote control from the hi-fi, and wondering why he can't get anything to work. Mr. Lawrence is on his phone to British Gas for an update. Grandad, having discovered which internal organs Mrs. Lawrence takes a professional interest in, is giving her a detailed history of his colon. Emma and I go and sit on the stairs. Everyone is wearing a two-colored paper hat. Even me.

It's cooler in the hall, out of the fog of the overcrowded living room. Already, on the stairs, you can catch the first whiffs of the Boxing Day Smell, the chilly aftertaste of cold vegetables and over-heated tempers. From the kitchen drifts the bump-clatter-clash of wash-and-dry combat. Emma and I sip fizzy stuff from our lunchtime wineglasses and play verbal dominoes. It's a game we devised while waiting to get into the art room, the first week we knew each other.

"Full words or acronyms?"

"Full words," says Emma. "Theme?"

"Ummm, families."

"I'll start," she says. "Mother."

"Relatives."

"Sister."

"R, r, r . . . rabbit."

"Rabbit?" says Emma.

"We had a rabbit once. It was one of the family."

"No, you can't have rabbit."

"I'm sorry about my lot," I blurt suddenly.

She smiles. "They're all right, aren't they? They're no worse than mine. You haven't met my uncle Matt's family."

"I hate Christmas," I mumble.

"Bah, humbug," says Emma in the deepest voice she can do. "Oh, come on, it's not that bad. It's all a bit of a giggle, isn't it?"

"It's all so . . . put on. Fake trees, fake snow, fake happiness. Why can't any of it be real? Why do we have to pretend there's a day in the year when everyone's nice to each other? Why can't we do it the rest of the time? Why can't people be nice to each other anyway?"

She leans over to me. Her face is very, very close to mine.

"You know," she says, almost in a whisper, "underneath it all, you're a soppy romantic like the rest of us, aren't you?"

For a second I look into those ice-clear blue eyes. They're saying so much, and all of it so quietly. I sit back suddenly.

Pressie! In a carefully prepared piece of spontaneity I reach behind myself and produce Emma's pressie. She sits back suddenly, and in a carefully prepared piece of spontaneity reaches behind herself and produces a pressie for me. They're in different wrapping papers, but they're both the same CD shape.

Emma laughs first. We swap.

"Happy Christmas, Dom."

I can't help but give her a broad smile. "Happy Christmas, Em."

In a comical flurry of fingers I rip the wrapping paper off my pressie. I turn it over and there's the cover of the rare German edition of Plastic's first single, long unavailable, much sought after by fans. Lisa Voyd blows an exaggerated kiss up at me.

"Wow," I say.

"I had to sneak behind your back and ask Tim what would be hard to track down. Hope you don't mind."

"No, no, course not. Wouldn't be a surprise then, would it? Wow."

"Well, I know you didn't go a bundle on the classical concert last birthday, so . . ."

She does a teeth-baring, shoulder-raising grin at me and tears neatly at the paper on her pressie. She holds it up. It's the rare German edition of Plastic's first single, long unavailable, much sought after by fans. Lisa Voyd blows an exaggerated kiss up at her.

"Ah!" she says. "Great minds think alike!"

"They're going up in value all the time," I say. "In a few years, you could sell it again for triple the money."

She raises a finger and her eyebrows. "Good investment!"

The gas leak gets fixed just before teatime.

"You are such an utter prat," says Lisa.

"Oh come on!" I protest. "That was the only copy I'd ever found!

I could have kept it to myself, but I gave it to her! It's already worth double what I paid for it, I was trying to be nice!"

(1:58 p.m. Lift time elapsed: ninety-one minutes.)

"You just don't get it, do you?" says Lisa, running a hand through her hair.

"What's there to get, for God's sake?"

"THINK ABOUT IT!"

A sudden metallic clang reverberates through the floor of the lift. We sit absolutely still for a moment.

"What the hell was that?" says Lisa quietly.

I twist to look down to the shop floor. A man and a woman, in gray overalls with a big yellow logo on the back, are fussing around at the base of the lift shaft. The security people are forming a loose barrier around them.

"The engineers are here," I say.

"At bloody last," says Lisa, almost to herself. Her face is in her hands.

I look back and see Emma in the crowd again. Tanya is still talking to the fan in the green pullover. Tim has an arm around Emma, but she's looking up at me. Those ice-clear blue eyes seem to expand towards me, and it suddenly feels like every atom of me is twisting uncomfortably.

I didn't get it, did I? I never really looked before, but now it's so sharply, hurtfully obvious that I'm more embarrassed than I've ever felt in my whole life.

I have to shift around, think about something else. Lisa is sitting very still, face still in hands.

"Are you OK?" I say at last.

She doesn't move. "Yeh. You just reminded me of last Christmas, that's all."

"I'm thinking happy thoughts
I'm thinking positively
I'm as happy as can be
I'm a happy, happy me"

—"Happy Clappy," from the Plastic album *Highly Offensive*
(Voyd/Parkins © Cellophane Music Ltd)

Last Christmas, says Lisa, when Emma's family were at your house, and I was on tour in the Far East with Plastic.

The main tower of the Lotus Palace Hotel, Bangkok, is circular and has twenty-seven floors. The top section is sloped and twisted. The whole thing looks like a giant fountain pen sticking up out of the city. The Plastic entourage are on floor 22, rooms 2210 to 2223. There are security guards stationed at each end of the corridor, at the lifts, and down in the lobby. None of them has encountered a psychopathic killer.

Meanwhile, I'm in room 2211. It's a room like any other in the hotel. It's a room like any other in any expensive hotel anywhere in the world. The only thing that reminds me I'm in Thailand is the strange choice of wallpaper. Giant green swirls. This is not a room to get drunk in.

The bed is opposite the window. There are big lamps on each side of the bed. There is a big TV and a big fridge and a big bathroom. Outside the window twinkle the late-night lights of the hotels and the bars.

This room is Bangkok. Bangkok is this room. This is where I am stored while I'm not at work. The record company execs and the tour promoters won't let me out on my own. If I really HAVE to go shopping or visit the city's temples, they say, then I MUST be accompanied by the security guards. But if I'm guarded, if they ring ahead to clear the way for me, if they keep the tourists at a safe distance, then I'm not really shopping, or visiting the city's temples, am I? I'm making a personal appearance. I'm making a point. I'm looking for a photo opportunity.

I can't go on my own. So I stay put, in this room. It's Christmas Eve. The other members of the band have gone out—with security guards, and tour managers, and a dozen other people I've never seen before and don't know the names of—to a nightclub in the city center. It's an exclusive, expensive place where they won't get pestered by fans.

I didn't go because I can't stand places like that. Even when they're exclusive and expensive I still get the ATTENTION. It's less blatant, that's all. It's whispers and nods instead of waves and shouts. And anyway, the other reason I didn't go was because they didn't ask me.

I'm sitting on the edge of the bed, on sheets laundered to within an inch of their lives. I flick through the TV channels, but it's all a parade of hysterical noise.

I sit still for a while, I don't know how long. It's quiet in here. I don't feel like moving. I'm very, very tired. My life exists in two time frames at once: whip fast and absolute stop. I can't adjust to either.

I'm so . . . tired. I go into the big bathroom and run a big bath. I'm getting used to it now, but having a bath in a hotel room in a distant city is the loneliest thing on earth. It's not restful or comforting. All it makes you feel is homesick.

By the time I'm back on the bed, wrapped in the hotel-logo bathrobe, it's nearly midnight. Nearly Christmas.

I lean on the windowsill and look down at the lights, with my head against the glass and my right foot twisted around my left leg. Thai people have a thing about feet. They're unclean, or something. You must never point your feet at the Buddha when you're visiting a temple.

So I've read.

My breath steams the glass in big droplet shapes. Today I've done a press junket, a record store signing, three radio interviews, two TV interviews, four different performances of the same song in four different studios in front of four different audiences. Me and Plastic.

And now it all stews in my head, like thick grease you can't scrape out of a pan. All this rubbish, all this STUFF. Faces, smiles, hands, light flashes, rooms, doors, the street, yells, waves, hellos, the back of a car, dark glass, street, glass doors, rooms, clacking boots on polished surfaces . . .

"Are you happy to be on tour, guys?"

"I read in the papers about you, Lisa. . . ."

"Are you working on your next album?"

And I smile, and I smile, and I smile, and I speak, and I speak nothing and nowhere to nobody. It makes sense at the time, and then it's gone. And they're looking at me. And it's never the same look twice. Everyone, looking at me.

"Are you happy to be on tour, guys?"

"I read in the papers about you, Lisa. . . ."

"Are you working on your next album?"

There's a shell called Lisa Voyd. An exterior, carefully assembled by others, glued together to a formula, oiled with publicity, glittered, polished, and shiny. Lisa Voyd is a product, to be bought off a shelf, copy after copy after copy of her, cloned, stamped, owned.

"Are you happy to be on tour, guys?"

"I read in the papers about you, Lisa. . . ."

"Are you working on your next album?"

People thrive on it, sometimes, for real. Famous people. Sometimes, it's what fuels them. You're in the Famous Club, where everyone's your friend, and anyone who doesn't make the grade is just a nobody. The Famous Club makes life worth living! Everyone wants to join! Free toys for qualifying members!

I'm famous. Yeeeaaa! I'm famous! Hey, then you meet other Famous Club members. Some of them are happy and hollow, like chocolate Santas. Some of them are little wooden puppets. Some of them are rare birds' eggs, stolen from their mother's nest. Some of them are poisonous. All of them, all of us club members, wear a skin of newsprint and spit wrapped around our faces. It's our uniform. It's what makes us who we are.

110

But we always have our friends, right? We always have our family, our loved ones?

The first boyfriend I ever had, when I was fifteen, was called Wayne. Funny name, spotty chin, the loveliest smile I'd ever seen. Soon after I joined the Famous Club, he got a pile of cash for telling the papers all about my school days and giving them photos of me he'd taken on a school trip. I heard through my mum that he bought himself a really nice car. I hadn't thought about him in ages, not in years even. But I thought about him a lot after that. It was my brother who dug those photos out, sorted through a dusty box in what had once been my room, handed them over, and took his share of the profits.

Every word I say is overheard by someone, and commented on, and misinterpreted by someone else. But they're my friends, right? I can trust them, can't I? The people from the record company, the people from the PR company, the people from the studios, the people who interview me, the people who maintain eye contact with me, the people who are doing their jobs. They're part of the Plastic machine. They're part of the money, part of the product. They're my friends, aren't they?

When I was growing up, all I wanted was music. Sound powered my heart and fed my mind. You're right, Dominic, music is very personal. It means different things to different people. To you it means belonging. To me it means knowing I exist.

Writing songs was always my first love; my voice was just a means to try out sounds. So already we were out of alignment, me and Fate. When I signed up with Plastic I was so happy, so looking forward to CREATING something. Then they gave me a vocal coach and a personal stylist. They told me to lose weight and look up when I walked.

But then, just when I can't believe how lonely I feel, suddenly there's a flash of contact, a flash of love. I'm standing on a stage.

I remember that night at the NEC clearly, that concert you were at, out there in the dark. I sing, because it's all that's left of me, and the whole crowd wants to hear. They're here for me, and the music, and when you all sing back I feel as if my heart will burst. The mass, collective joy of the moment holds me tight and keeps me safe. The sound and the crowd are the whole world, and it's a world that's pure and loving, just for a little while. It's the most wonderful feeling. It's so wonderful.

You can see it in a single face, sometimes. For a split second, here and there, a face in a jostling crowd in the street, or in the eyes of a fan who suddenly sees you close up, without expecting it. That wonderful sense of something beyond. It was in your eyes, Dominic, down on the shop floor.

And then it's lost again. It collapses and decays, as if one person can't contain it. It gets too personal, too needy, too close.

So I sink backwards into the voices and the noise. I sit on a bed in a hotel room in a distant place, and I wonder to myself why I ever allowed it all to happen. It was going to be so exciting, so much what I wanted, so much part of the BIG PLAN. And I hate it, despite those moments of joy. And I'm so very tired.

"Are you happy to be on tour, guys?"

"I read in the papers about you, Lisa. . . ."

"Are you working on your next album?"

"Are you happy to be on tour, guys?"

"I read in the papers about you, Lisa. . . ."

"Are you working on your next album?"

It never stops. It never, ever stops. Even in this hotel room, this silence, this absolute halt, it's still screaming through me. Move on, move on, next, next, next, next, and it's all such bloody RUBBISH.

Every day there's something else. There's always a rumor to print, and a lie to spread. There's always another picture to take. They don't care what they say about me. It's not their job to care. It's just their job to say it anyway.

I can't filter it out. I can't dismiss it, or let it go. It's a skill I haven't got, and the lack of it is drowning me. I damn well DO care when some greasy columnist I've never met starts spitting hate about my clothes, my hair, my past, my future, my life. What bloody RIGHT have they got?

I can't peel off my public skin. Some members of the club can, but I can't. And if you're one of those who can't, your life will eat you. Slow and raw. Some members of the club defend themselves from it all by growing giant egos, by taking command of those around them in any way they can. I can't do that either. It makes me feel ridiculous.

I never wanted all this. All I wanted was the feeling of the music.

Plastic aren't the greatest band in the world. We're OK, sometimes we're pretty good, but we're not great. We can play catchy tunes and get people dancing, but will anybody be listening to what we've done in a hundred years' time? In the howling, flashing hurricane of pop culture, what are we? A tiny part of a tiny part of nothing very much. Even in the club there are losers and nobodies, in the end.

I don't think Plastic will last much longer. Sean, and Kurt, and Mike, and me. Surprised? Every band has its shock-horror breakup rumors. Ours have finally got a grain of truth in them.

Why? It didn't take long for the rest of Plastic to start resenting my presence. Name a male band with a female singer? I could name you dozens. But take the singer away, and how many people would know which band was which?

I'm the one who gets the MOST attention, you see. I'm Plastic, I'm the product. I'm the one who doesn't need a backstage security pass. I'm the one who gets shouted at from the crowd, and looked at by everyone, and talked about by the press. I'm the one who gets put on magazine covers. I'm the one who gets faked pictures of her posted on the Net. I live in a tiny goldfish bowl, going round and round and round, all magnified and golden.

You can't really blame them for not liking me much anymore. I'm the one who seems to get the best deal from my Club membership.

Kurt's the worst, usually. He's never exactly been the most polite of sorts, but more often than not these days he just pretends I'm not in the room. It doesn't usually amount to too much of a problem. I just ignore him back. It keeps the peace.

Sean always wants to do more "serious" work. Heavier rock 'n' roll, dressed in more leather and longer hair. It's a terrible idea. It's dated and it wouldn't suit any of us. He keeps having screaming rows with Bob Fullbright and the record company. I'd almost be grateful for the fights if they drew press attention away from me for a while, but they don't. Pop stars are allowed to be "difficult." It's not news. Mike and I are rather surprised that Sean hasn't left the band already. I think he's afraid to jump. I think he's scared of leaving the club.

Mike is someone I used to like a lot. I do the words, he does the notes, and it all fits OK. So we must be doing something right. He's very like me in a lot of ways, but he got lost in it all very quickly. In all the noise of this dazzling lifestyle choice.

He went through a phase when he'd only eat things which were white. Bread, sugar, milk, egg whites. Vanilla ice cream was acceptably pale. It only lasted a few weeks. It gave him stomach cramps. That night at the NEC he said he was in agony.

Sometimes he says the oddest things. He'll stop a conversation with a sudden off-the-wall remark, and then stand there smirking while everyone else just looks at each other. Sometimes I think he's lost the ability to understand how things work. Sometimes he'll stare at a page in a magazine for hours. Sometimes I find him sitting on the stairs or in a corner, sobbing his heart out, and he won't know why.

The three of them are out tonight, Christmas Eve. Christmas Day! And none of them wanted me tagging along. Tomorrow—no, today—there's breakfast with our PR managers, then I'm doing Euro-Yuletide food on some stupid TV cookery show ("Lisa, luv, it'll do well with the over-thirties"), then we're miming to our new single for a live satellite link to Scandinavia, then all the Plastic crew are having a Christmas dinner in a private function room at the hotel (which will turn into a bloody awful food fight and a drinking contest because Bob Fullbright and Kurt are there), then there's rehearsals for the next day's—tomorrow's—concert at a place on the edge of the city . . .

I curl up on the bed and try to close some of it out.

I'm so tired.

But I can't sleep.

TRACK NINE

"It's a long way down that road, they say
I'm going to go there anyway"

—"You, Me and the Dog," from the Plastic album *Highly Offensive*
(Voyd/Parkins © Cellophane Music Ltd)

2:12 p.m. Lift time elapsed: one hundred and five minutes.

Lisa puffs out her cheeks and blows, slowly, like a gently deflating balloon. She rubs at her face, as if she's expecting it to slide off to give her skull room to breathe.

"So . . . is this Christmas going to be any better?" I say quietly. I'm feeling as if a giant rock dropped on top of me: ever so slightly stunned. My mind has pins and needles.

She pauses. She doesn't look at me. "They've promised us a fortnight," she says. "But it won't happen. The marketing parasites have been whining about slipping sales. Down four percent. Panic stations. If you want to boost your bottom line all you've got to do is fire the marketing parasites, that's what I said. Went down like a cup of cold sick."

"But it's not all bad. You said so yourself."

"Oh, sure. There are times. And the money's good," she says.

"Surely any real achievement is worth working hard for?"

She suddenly fixes me with a dismissive stare. "How would you know? What have you ever achieved? I thought your life was Plastic?"

"Well, if it's THAT awful," I shout angrily, "give it up! Give it ALL UP!"

My throat tries to claw back the words, but it's too late.

Holy goddam cow, I've told Lisa Voyd to give it up!

"And do what? Dominic? Eh? I've never had an ordinary, straight-forward job in my whole life. I joined Plastic straight from school. I couldn't cut it in the real world. I'd end up on the makeup counter at some department store, getting sniggered at and hearing bloody stupid jokes about failed careers!"

"But . . . You're in Plastic. You ARE great. Plastic ARE great. That's the achievement of a lifetime, isn't it?"

Holy goddam cow, I've told Lisa Voyd to give it up!

"We're a band, Dominic. Oh sure, in the world of early twenty-first-century British four-piece female-lead-singer rock-pop groups, we're giants. Giants! We mean everything to YOU, because YOU close yourself off from the rest of what's going on. I can't turn back from the choices I've made, and I hate it with a passion I can't begin to express. And you. You WASTE so much. You make me sick."

The pins and needles in my mind twist up and go rusty. She . . . why . . . I can't . . .

"But . . . Lisa . . . I know you wouldn't—"

"You don't know anything. You don't know me. You know Public Me. You know Plastic Me. Someone I don't like spending time with anymore." She rocks forward onto her knees and crawls towards me, keeping out of sight of the shop floor below as much as possible.

She's very close to me. I can feel the movement of her breath against my cheek. I can't return her gaze. I see every contoured hair of her eyebrows, a tiny blemish to one side of her nose, a delicate line of skin upon her upper lip, disguised with lipstick. Suddenly, I'm terrified.

"What would you do," she says, "if I gave it all up? What would you do without me and Plastic?"

She watches me closely for a second or two. Very closely. This is Lisa Voyd, goddess of cool. Public Lisa. Plastic Lisa. I don't know anymore. She retreats to her corner.

I turn and look down. The lift engineers are on the other side of the shop with the shop manager and Bob Fullbright, by the door the shop manager was keeping locked before. The door's open, and I can see a wall covered in cabling and electrical junction boxes.

The truth about why we're stuck here finally dawns on me: the shop manager's furtiveness, that locked door, Bob Fullbright's attitude . . .

Tanya and Tim are busy. Tanya has squeezed her way through the crowd and is closer to the entrance now, several glaring lights pointed in her direction. She's being interviewed by one of the camera crews. I recognize the woman with the microphone. I've seen her reporting on rock music award ceremonies and disgraced Hollywood stars.

Tim is busy with Emma. He has an arm around her. They are talking, earnestly, intimately.

I feel like my insides are draining away. I want to get out of here.
I want to get out of this lift. I've changed my mind. Now, suddenly,
I want to get out.

He's got his arm around her. Perhaps he's telling her the things I
said about her, that stuff I really didn't mean. If he does, she'll never
speak to me again. She'll despise me forever. I'm surprised she
doesn't already.

She's all yours, I told him. You're welcome to her.

(*"So she's dull, hysterical and has issues,"* says Tim. *"And she's perfect
for me."*

"Right.")

I want to get out. I want to GET OOOOOUUUT!

"If you're the sunshine of my life Oh hell, I'm in a lot of strife"

—"No Way, Babe," lyrics by Dominic "Sherlock" Smith, unpublished, stuck away in a drawer where they belong

"Why sixteen pages?" says Emma.

"Because when they send this out to the printer's, it's got to fit a certain number of pages or it gets more expensive. Something to do with the big sheets of paper that go into the printing presses, I'm told."

We've known each other awhile. A couple terms or so. We're at the computer that's tucked into a corner of her parents' living room, because (1) we volunteered to assemble the school magazine this term (i.e., we were ordered at emotional gunpoint by our form tutor to assemble the school magazine this term), and (2) her dad's got a nifty page layout application that came free with the computer.

We give each other an exaggerated, droopy-mouthed shrug. OK, sixteen pages it is. Quite how we're going to turn a box file full of scribbled rubbish into sixteen pages of scintillating prose, I don't know.

Emma's slowly leafing through the file. Most of the pieces of paper are either slightly crumpled (the more junior pupil news submissions) or slightly tea-stained (the more senior pupil news submissions). The rest are handwritten in worryingly colorful inks (the teacher submissions).

"I don't know where to start," says Emma, wrinkling her nose at the paper pile. It's Sunday afternoon, but she's dressed in the same outfit I know she wore to the work experience day she did at a legal office in town. She exudes a freshly soapy smell which makes me self-conscious about the frying pan state of my hair.

I take the box file from her lap and start setting the papers out across the thickly sound-deadening carpet. You can tell how posh this carpet is by the way the papers kind of float on the tips of the fibers.

Not quite like at home. At this precise moment, Gran is shampooing mud out of the hall floor, following Seb's rendition of Superheroes Versus Godzilla Pro-Am Indoor-Outdoor Garden Golf World Cup. ("Hole in one!" "No, you miniature troll, that's a hole in thirty-six." "Hole in one!")

It's very quiet in Emma's living room. The tick-clunk of the grandfather clock drifts in from the hall. Outside the bay windows, the outer branches of trees swirl gently.

I give a couple of sniffs and clap my hands together. "OK," I say at last, having given the problem some thought, "you're on typography and page-space-organizing duties, I'm on giving all this stuff a thump up the paragraphs."

"Aye-aye."

"Work that mouse, babe!"

Surprisingly, it only takes us a couple of hours. Emma's innate sense of order gets things regimented into standard format, and my innate sense of how to sort out crap sentence structure gets things translated from the original gibberish. I stand there with each sheet of paper in turn and dictate something which makes more sense, while Emma does her touch-typing bit and flows text around the gaps where the photos will go.

When we're finished, I lean over her chair and peer at the screen. "Zap," I say quietly. "Kapow."

"I thought that was going to take us halfway to Monday," she says.

"Ah, we make a sensational team," I say, as Emma saves the file onto a CD.

She turns to look at me. "Don't we just," she says softly.

"Do you like my new T-shirt?" I say, standing back to let her admire it properly.

"Err, it's black and it has Plastic on it," she says. "How exactly is it different from all your other T-shirts?"

I draw a square outline in the air in front of my chest. "Album cover," I say.

"Ooookay."

The computer ejects the CD and Emma clicks it into a case she's got ready-labeled. She holds it up. "Are you going to give this in tomorrow, or shall I?"

"You do it. I might forget to put it in my bag. You won't."

She stares at my T-shirt. It's certainly darned impressive.

She waggles the disc at me. "You ought to do more of this," she says. "You're so good at it."

"And, arr, you're a whiz at the keyboard."

"I'm not fishing for compliments, dumbo, I mean it. You've got a real gift for words. You stood there making it up as you went along. That's something I couldn't do in a million years."

I don't really get her point. "What, you mean I should volunteer for this every term?"

"Well, no, not necessarily. I mean writing in general. I dunno, journalism, novels, whatever."

"Oh God, don't start on about long-term goals, you'll sound like my mother."

"I'm not! I'm just saying you'd make a good writer."

I purse my lips and gaze out of the window for a moment or two. I'm pondering something.

"What?" she says.

"Aaaaactually," I say, not sure I want to be saying this at all, "it's funny you should say that. . . ."

She smiles like she can't help it. "Why?"

"Weeell . . . I do write a few . . . lyrics, occasionally."

"Really?" she cries, unable to help herself squeezing up on her chair in delight. "What, like poetry?"

"No!" I protest. "POETRY? Good grief, what kind of weed do you take me for? Song lyrics! It's not the same thing at all."

"Can be."

"No it can't."

"Can I read them?"

"Umm . . . Actually, I . . . carry most of them around in my head. There's no music to them! Don't expect me to sing or anything!"

"No, no, that's fine, great, go on, please, I'd love to hear them."

I can't believe I'm doing this. I've never told anyone, ANYONE, about my lyrics, not even Tim and Tanya. I feel slightly silly. But I can't take it back now.

I look out of the window and watch the tree branches, which is much easier than focusing on anything in the room. "They're, err, heavily ironic, you know, like the song lyrics of Lisa Voyd. . . . Umm . . . With a bit of a dark edge to them . . . There's one called 'Animals,' which starts . . . *There's blood on the carpet, where once it was sat, those terrible children, have murdered the cat.* . . . And it goes on about beasts and things. . . . And there's one about a kid who's struggling with his feelings, you know, he's in a lot of pain. . . . *Love ya girl, yeah, love ya girl, I swear, nothing can compare, losing u I couldn't bear.* . . . That's *u* as in the letter *u*, not *y-o-u* because the kid is, you know, quite street. . . . *This isn't fair, I only stare, you're in the glare, of what you wear.* . . ."

I turn to face her. She's crumpled up on the side of the sofa, red in the face, with her hands clamped over her mouth, trying not to laugh.

"What's wrong with them?"

The dam bursts. "Haaaaaa HAAAAAAAAAAAAAAAA ha ha HAAAAAAAAAAA!"

"They're very personal."

125

"They're very bad," she squeaks in a high-pitched strangle. "Haaaa haaa ha ha ha ha ha ha HAAAAAAAAAAA!"

"Thanks."

Eventually she just about composes herself. She speaks in a controlled squark that's about to erupt into a scream at any moment. "Oh, Dominic, I'm really really sorry, I don't mean to laugh, really."

"So I'd make a good writer, would I?"

She flaps a hand at me. "Yes, yes you would, please don't let me put you off—"

"Perish the thought. . . ."

"—but it's just that obviously poetry isn't your thing. At all. Try novels!"

"It's not poetry."

"Lyrics! Lyrics, I'm so sorry, please, I don't mean to upset you but . . . really, you've got to see the funny side of it. . . ."

"They're very personal."

"Oh, Dominic, I'm sorry," she says, wiping tears from her eyes. "Where's a tissue? Have you got many more?"

". . . A few."

"Oh please, please, please let me hear them. HA HA HAAAAAAAAAAA!"

"Aural inner space comes pressed, I'll love you in my sitting room, I think"

—"Yours for a Tenner," from the Plastic album *Highly Offensive*
(Voyd/Parkins © Cellophane Music Ltd)

2:19 p.m. Lift time elapsed: one hundred and twelve minutes.

The engineers are back at work on the mechanism beneath the lift. I keep watching them as best I can, but they move out of sight a lot, their overalls rippling as the angle of the edges of the glass distorts them. But I keep watching, as if my watching them will hurry them up. I want to get out of here.

Lisa is getting impatient too. The toe of her boot tap-tap-taps on the glass wall beside her. The air in here has become heavy and treacled.

Down on the shop floor the security guards are herding the crowd as far back as the crowd can be herded. There's a quickening of movement here and there, a definite rise in the level of ambient noise that comes through the glass to me, dulled and fogged. Something's happening, or something's expected to happen.

The lift's lights blink on and off. The effect is so sudden that both of us flinch. We look at each other in silence.

There's a steady bleeping sound coming from below the lift. The lights brighten and dull, then steady themselves like a tightrope walker. I've got used to having stark areas of shadow in here, and I find myself shielding my eyes from the glare above and below me. Lisa's shape is contoured with a new set of shadows now she's illuminated from beneath.

A grinding thump-thump-thump of mechanisms shakes the lift. Then it slips down a few centimeters. There's a scream of crowd-sound from outside.

"Jeeesus," says Lisa, hands to the floor.

I hate to admit it, but I'm starting to get nervous. I have no idea why, because I don't have any fear that the lift will fall—they only do that in the movies. Even so, surrounded by glass and however-many meters off the ground, I'm starting to get nervous.

I swing around and search for Emma, Tanya and Tim in the crowd. I can spot only Tanya, being pushed back by security guards. She sees me looking and throws up a hand at me, fingers splayed.

"Five minutes," I say quietly. "They say we'll be out in five minutes."

"OK," whispers Lisa. Her eyes are aimed at the ceiling. She's thinking what I've been thinking. So I think about something else. I backtrack to this morning.

The events of today: a countdown.

7 a.m. My eyes snap open. "And that's the headlines, we're looking at a heavy frost across most parts of the country, cloud and scattered

showers moving in from the west, with the outlook for more of the same, you're listening to EMR on ninety-nine point eight FM and deeee aaaay beeee. Here's Plastic's latest at nearly two minutes past seven."

I smile to myself. It's fate, Plastic coming on like that. Today of all days. I snake a hand out from under the covers and switch the thing off. Once the track's finished.

7:22 a.m. "No, Dad, I'm afraid it's news to me," says Mum.

"Hmm, I don't think so, Mum," says Dad. "I have actually been part of the weekend rota at work for nearly four years."

"Well, perhaps it might be courteous to remind us in advance when your turn comes round?"

"I'm terribly sorry, I'll print it in Day-Glo lettering on the fridge, shall I?"

I'm eating cornflakes. Seb is eating an orange mush which used to be cornflakes until he customized it into Special Crushed Up Action Man Toxic Waste Cornflakes instead. Action Man looks on, unimpressed.

"Dominic."

"Mmm?"

"You'll be here all morning, won't you? To keep an eye on Seb."

"No, I'm going to Birmingham with Tim and Tanya. I said last week. Why do you think I'm up at seven on a Saturday?"

"Oh. Well, I'm sorry, you'll have to go another day."

"No no no, we're going to a signing session. We can't go another day. I said last week."

Mum does one of her all-over bird twitches. "I'm sorry, Dominic,"

129

she says. "I have to go into work, Dad all of a sudden has to go into work and Gran is taking Grandad to the doctor's. You'll have to stay here."

"It's NOT all of a sudden," says Dad.

"Muuum! Why can't Seb go with Gran?"

"No way," burbles Seb through a mouthful of toxic waste. "That place smells."

"Gran has to look after Grandad," says Mum, clearly not believing a word she's saying.

I drop my spoon into the bowl. "Mum, Lisa Voyd is signing copies of the new Plastic album at Big Deal Records and I am not, not, NOT going to miss it!"

"So a pop star is more important than your brother?" snaps Mum.

"Infinitely!"

"The place will be swarming with pickpockets! You won't get to see a thing."

"I don't care! I'm going!"

7:58 a.m. Dad has been forced to take Seb with him to work. I'm at the station, waiting for the 8:02 to Moor Street. Tim is sauntering up and down the platform, swinging his carrier bag. Tanya is doing silent dance moves and getting funny looks from other travelers.

Emma is waiting for the same train, standing as close to me as etiquette allows. It's been exactly a week since she locked me in the equipment room and ruined the whole Plastic Bag thing. I'm still barely speaking to her.

Of course, she's not going to the signing. She's going into Birmingham to her Saturday job, at one of the bookshops in the Bullring shopping mall. She twists on the spot as she waits, and the way she's keeping me under surveillance couldn't be more obvious if she were standing on my toes with her nose against mine.

"What time does it start?" she says.

My thoughts are elsewhere and it takes me a second to answer. "Twelve."

She does a slow nod. "I bet it'll be pretty crowded."

I grunt. Long pause.

8:19 a.m. We're on the train, counting off the stations. Warwick Parkway, Dorridge, Solihull, Widney Manor . . . closer and closer. Tim and Tanya and I are pretty cool about the whole thing, though. Hey, we're USED to being a part of the Plastic world. We've seen them in CONCERT already. But this'll be . . . closer and closer.

Tanya points out numerological links between the cities on the last Plastic tour of the Far East. Tim's brought a printout of the overnight postings to the Web site. Tanya's halfway through reading it when she slaps the paper and gasps.

"Holy cow, Trackerman!"

Tim nods quickly and grins. He's been waiting for Tanya to spot this.

"Who?" says Emma, perched on the seat by the window. A burst of run-down rail maintenance buildings flashes past behind her.

"The guy who faked himself into that Plastic video," says Tanya. "He's done it again!"

"Wow, what's he done now?" I say.

Tim nudges his glasses back up his nose. "He took a movie teaser trailer off a Hollywood site and pasted Lisa's face over the main character. Fantastic results, you'd swear it was her. She blasts these people into strawberry jam, blood everywhere."

"Doesn't she mind?" says Emma quietly. "I'd mind."

"Ha!" I cry. "He'll have two sets of lawyers after him!"

"Already has," says Tim, his grin threatening to split his face in two. "They blocked all access to his Web host, then they blocked the backup site he posted through one of the search engine freebie hosts. All in half an hour. It's really hit the fan. That trailer is dead and buried, online."

He's still grinning. Tanya edges towards him. She's grinning too, now. "But . . . you got it, didn't you?" she says with suppressed glee.

Tim nods. "Seconds to spare. I thought my connection would be cut off, but I just made it." He slides his hand through the air like it was missing a sharply descending wall of steel. Tanya squeaks, flings her arms around his neck and plants a whopping kiss on his forehead.

"You're a little genius," she says.

Tim folds in at the edges. He's still grinning. "I know. I know."

*   *   *

$8:40$ a.m. The train pulls into Moor Street and emits a few dozen passengers. We're quietly pleased that we appear to be the only Plastic fans among them. I glance up and down the platform: no Plastic sweatshirts, no Lisa hairstyles. For whatever reason, it's the first time the three of us have managed to get to one of these personal appearance things, but it looks like we've judged it about right.

We hurry up the tarmac slope that leads away from the station. Across a huge road, along a walkway, across a small road, under an arched area and we're into the undulating, white-paved expanse of the Bullring. Vertical slices of city can be seen between the steel and glass. In one of the gaps looms the sci-fi weirdness of the Selfridges building. We head to the right, to Big Deal Records, just out of sight around the corner.

"See ya then!"

Huh?

Emma is waving from a few meters away, and pointing to one of the buildings opposite. "I'm this way."

"Oh, right, see ya!" call Tim and Tanya.

We turn the corner. Oh rats hellfire dammit and bum!

The crowd gathered outside the shop is already of a size that makes the turnout at the school concert look like an intimate dinner party.

*   *   *

11:34 a.m. It's taken two and a half hours, but through a combination of slow shuffling, people-standing-in-front-of-you distraction techniques and good old-fashioned pushing, the three of us have managed to worm our way to a spot close to the glass doors.

Inside the shop it is dark. I get the occasional glimpse of a yellow T-shirted person moving here and there, but nothing other than that.

Outside the shop, the air is cold and clear, with a sharply blue sky, one of those rare days in winter which seems pleasant and promising instead of miserably sad. The long wait has actually been fun so far, in an empty-headed sort of way. There's a slowly expanding buzz in the crowd that's building with every passing minute. Wristwatches and mobile phone clocks are getting looked at ever more frequently.

11:41 a.m. A gang of security guards is filtering out of a side entrance somewhere. They clearly think they look inconspicuous. They don't. I'm surprised that there aren't more of them. Surely there'd normally be more of them? This is Surprise No. 1 in a series of three.

11:47 a.m. The sound of the crowd swells suddenly. Heads all around us bob left and right, looking for a sign. The car's here, the car must be here.

We can't see it yet. The sound rises and rises, shifting from a general noise to distinct shouts and yells and cheers. The car must be here.

I catch a flash of light bouncing off glass. The car—it's a limo with darkened windows, what a fabulous cliché—is coming from the other side of the crowd. It must have driven up the huge road by the station and turned off along the normally pedestrianized underpass.

She's here.

"She's here!" squeals Tanya. Tim snaps open the cover on his camera.

The limo glides to a halt silently, the crowd drowning out the low growl of its engine. Camera flashes start to click click click click click click.

One of the glass doors of the shop swings open. A couple of yellow T-shirt types come out, with the baldy shop manager bustling behind. The security guards have cleared a path for Lisa, pushing back the crowd, but facing into it. There are just enough of them to reach from the limo to the shop. There's a crush of bodies around me. Someone's red coat is squashed against my shoulder, someone else's foot steps on mine.

The door of the limo swings open. A sudden rush of voices rises and falls as Bob Fullbright jumps out and crosses quickly to the shop manager. They've clearly met before. They don't greet each other like strangers—there are no handshakes. Surprise No. 2 in the series of three. It's strange that Plastic's manager would have taken the trouble to make arrangements for this himself. Or so it would seem from what I've read in the past. Surprise No. 3 is that he's actually here at all. Also not usually part of his remit. There's no army of PR clones either, just a couple of suits emerging from the other side of the car.

Cheers suddenly whirl into whoops and waves. I see the top of Lisa's head rise from behind the dark limo door. She stands. Her face. Her shape. It's her! Flash click flash click flash click flash click flash click.

"Lisa! Lisa!"

"Lisa! Over here!"

"I love you!"

"WhoooooooooAA!"

Hands, eyes, stretched-out fingers.

She waves back, she smiles and she's past us and into the shop. The guards group behind her, smoothly cutting off the crowd. They all disappear and the door is held shut by the T-shirts. The shop manager is standing on something I can't see, he's poking up a meter or so above the heads of the crowd. He has a small piece of paper in his hand, but not a single eye is on him and in a few moments he decides that his short speech of welcome can wait.

He drops down and indicates to someone inside. He's let in, squeezing through the gap. The cheers and calls don't subside for a single second.

11:58 a.m. Simultaneously, the center two of the half dozen glass doors of the shop are opened. The crowd surges forward. The yellow T-shirt brigade are at the doors in force, regulating the flow.

We all shuffle along. Tanya, Tim and I don't exchange a word. We don't need to. Gradually, like the sand in an hourglass, the crowd moves into the shop. As I cross the threshold I feel a blast of warm air from the heaters overhead.

I'm extremely impressed with this shop. You look up and see all three stories through chrome frames and colored glass. The atrium into which I'm being herded is enormous, all banners and shelves and projected images. The place is so tall I'm surprised the walls manage to reach the ceiling. There's a glass lift, close to where a wide table has been set up, and at which sits Lisa.

I tug at Tanya's sleeve and flick my head at the CD racks over to the right. She sees what I mean and tugs at Tim. Everyone's flowing the other way. Until it's spotted by others, there's an almost clear run skirting the perimeter of the shop floor around to the table.

"Go go go," says Tanya under her breath.

We dash fast enough to beat the movement of people, but not so fast as to draw unneccessary attention. In half a minute we're almost at the side of the table.

It occurs to me now that the surprisingly limited number of security guards here are having a tough time keeping things under control. The area around the table is far too wide for them to keep the crowd as far back as they want to. There are only a couple of people between me and Lisa. She doesn't seem worried—entirely her usual confident self. She's talking to someone at the front of the crowd, nodding and smiling. Flashes blink all over the place like photographic fairy dust.

The shop manager, standing behind the table, keeps nervously looking over at Bob Fullbright, who's got a smug, knowing look on his face. The security guards keep looking nervously at the shop manager. Eventually, after a final glance at Bob Fullbright, the shop manager claps his hands loudly and shouts above the now-subsiding din.

"If, umm, if I could have your attention, please, ladies and gentle-men!" The din subsides a little more. "I, umm, thank you for coming today to the grand opening of Big Deal Records, and, umm, to the fantastic Lisa Voyd—" His next couple of sentences are obliterated by the spontaneous cheer. "We, umm, there's such a lot of you here today at our grand opening, umm, that, umm, because we want everyone to get a proper chance to meet Lisa we're going to relo-cate the signing to the top floor of the shop, umm, if, umm, where there's more space. If you could, umm, bear with us just a few min-utes, umm, the top floor is where you'll find even more bargain prices, umm." Quick glance at Bob Fullbright. "Bear with us, ladies and gentlemen, thank you."

Lisa's playing it cool, not reacting to anything. She's talking to someone else now, further along. I catch a faint grumble from the crowd about rubbish organization.

The shop manager beckons and a couple of scruffy-headed guys emerge. They're wearing the standard yellow Big Deal T-shirts; they're back-room staff of some sort. Neither of them looks much older than me, and both of them look like they'd rather be some-where else. They pick up armfuls of CDs from the table and slope off towards the escalators that lead to the upper floors.

Bob Fullbright leans down to Lisa's ear. She nods and stands, moving back from the table. As she moves, so does the crowd. There's a fresh surge of noise and anticipation. People shuffle. The security guards are getting edgy. A small section of the crowd on the far side of the table balloons out in front of the others. With a series of doglike barks to each other, the guards close in to round up the strays.

My side of the crowd is left momentarily unguarded. I feel sharp nudges from behind. I've lost track of Tim and Tanya. Half a dozen, including me, slide right up to the table. I'm the tallest of them.

Slow motion.

Lisa is moving to follow the guys with the CDs, her flap-ankled jeans flowing. She notices a stack they've left behind. The shop manager throws another quick glance at Bob Fullbright, then takes Lisa's elbow in one hand and points her towards the lift with the other. A shout from one of the guards draws him away.

Lisa looks back at the CDs, and the movement of her head brings me slap bang into her line of sight. Me, with my yellow T-shirt.

"Hey, bring those, willya? They're ones I've signed for your colleagues."

I don't hesitate, not for the merest fraction of a split second. I'm standing right there. She thinks I'm one of the back-room guys. Bring the CDs, she says. So I do.

The guards are occupied. I follow her closely, into the lift. It only takes a second. I glance back. The shop manager, now a few meters away beside the crowd-wrangling guards, reaches out at me with a violently alarmed look on his face. I ignore him. No hesitation. I hear a shout from Bob Fullbright, somewhere over by the table.

Lisa presses the large, round 3 button. As I step into the lift I turn on my heels. The crowd, awash with smiles and searching looks, gushes at the glass doors as they slide shut. A sharp ping sounds.

The noise is cut in half. I catch a brief glimpse of Tim and Tanya, random faces in the mass.

The lift glides up. Then the lights flicker. Something klunks in the mechanism above us. The lift shudders to a halt, halfway between floors. The lights go out. Lisa starts stabbing at the buttons in frustration.

12:27 p.m.

2:29 p.m. The lift lurches again. Lisa spits out two words, each of which contains four letters. We look at each other all over again.

Very slowly, the lift begins to descend. An almighty cheer rises from below us. I look out at Tim and Tanya: two beaming expressions, four thumbs-up signs.

Emma is watching nervously. She looks pale. At least she's still here.

I don't know what to think. I have no idea, just at this precise moment, exactly what could or should or might be going through my head. I know what I would have thought two hours ago. But that was then, as they say, and this is now.

"Oh God," says Lisa quietly. "Here we go."

She's standing with her hands out to her sides, flat against the back of the lift. She seems . . . caged. She seems like a child and an old woman all at the same time. I'm feeling a whole new set of emotions, as if I've just upgraded my insides and haven't got used to them yet.

"Get ready," she says, almost in a whisper. "When the doors open, all hell will break loose. Welcome to my world, Mr. Smith."

"It doesn't have to be like this," I say. "Go back to writing songs, like you always wanted."

She doesn't look away from the doors. The lift is only a couple of meters off the ground floor now. "You don't suddenly give all this up. That's not how it works."

I try reverse psychology. "I think you're scared."

She hesitates. Thoughts tussle for control of her face. "Of course I'm scared. I'm scared of turning myself into a joke. I'm scared of being second-rate. People will do anything to get where I am, to have what I've got. If you give up that kind of power, that kind of in- fluence, then what are you? What's left of you?"

Security guards have formed a barrier in front of the lift doors, their backs pressed tight to the glass. We're all but out of sight, for the few seconds remaining.

"You're Lisa Voyd," I say. "You're the living embodiment of style and self-assurance. You know how much Plastic means to all of us out there, but if it's part of the past, then say so. Don't let it fall apart. Leave it perfect and complete. We'll all just have to learn to move on, won't we?"

The lift is almost down. There's an unearthly hush across the shop.

She reaches out and holds my hand. "Give my love to Emma."

She stands up straight in front of the doors. New again. Lisa Voyd. The public Lisa Voyd, the take-no-prisoners Lisa Voyd who makes a million hearts sing.

The lift stops. There's a sharp ping, and the doors slide open.

"Tell it, tell me, tell them all
Hide it at your peril, little people"

—"What's Past Is Processed," from the Plastic album *Highly Offensive*
(Voyd/Parkins © Cellophane Music Ltd)

The noise . . .

. . . is beyond everything.

The lights are above us, blinding, washing out the faces of the pressing crowd.

Hands pull at me, and pull at her.

"What happened, Lisa?"

"Lisa!"

"This way, Lisa!"

"Lisa!"

"How do you feel, Lisa?"

"Lisa!"

"Did he try anything, Lisa?"

"Lisa!"

"How do you feel, Lisa?"

Voices and people and lights on top of each other. It's like a bucket of hot water thrown in your face. I nearly overbalance. Security guards shove people aside. Shouts bounce around like ricocheting bullets.

Lisa stands with her hands held high, standing still while cameras machine-gun-click away. Microphones are thrust out at her, most of them collared with radio and TV station logos. Questions attack her from all sides. Her face is controlled, her expression mildly amused. Her exterior self is as breathtaking as ever. The mask is total.

Suddenly, I'm pulled aside sharply. Fingers are digging into my upper arm. The shop manager's face appears huge and bulbous right beside mine.

"Who the HELL are you? You're right in it, you are, boy!" I can see the dimples in his forehead and smell his breath.

I catch a lightning glimpse of Bob Fullbright, passing behind an assortment of heads and shoulders. His face is cooked to the same recipe of hardened hostility as the shop manager's.

All the oddities of the past couple of hours have clicked together in my head pretty neatly by now. Dominic "Sherlock" Smith speaks. "Who am I? I'm the one who's rumbled your and Bob Fullbright's little publicity stunt."

The manager lets go of my arm as if it's poisonous. The hostility in his face swells into hatred and then slumps back into simple horror like a deflating pudding.

"WHAT?" he spits. Actually spits. A fleck of it lands on his chin.

"The low level of security, the 'unexpected' need to move the signing upstairs, the way you were guarding access to that room over there, which I presume contains the lift's power supply controls, the time it took to call the engineers, the way you haven't had this shop cleared of people, it all adds up. You've got a new business to publicize and Bob Fullbright's getting jittery over CD sales. Do I need to go on?"

The manager stares at me. "You snotty little—"

"Only I'm the fly in the ointment, aren't I."

"If you DARE—"

"Why don't you stop worrying about me and look after Lisa?"

He thrusts me aside and barges his way through the crowd. "Dominic!"

Emma squeezes the slightness of her frame between two security guards at their waist level, and I feel—I'm conscious that I feel—much better for seeing her. She flings her arms around me and I hold her to me.

"Dominic! Are you all right?"

"I'm fine, I'm fine!"

Her mouth is stuck on fast forward. "It was on the news on the radio in the bookshop staff room I couldn't believe it and Tanya had told the news crews who you were and when they said it I thought it was just typical of you to go getting yourself into something like that over Plastic and—"

"Hey, hang on, I'm fine, it's all over, OK?"

She lets out a semihuff and transfixes me with those eyes of hers. "Don't you dare do that again! You are the biggest berk of all time, Dominic Smith," she gasps.

"I know. I'm so pleased to see you."

She gazes at me for what appears to be about a year and a half, and I gaze back.

"Are you?" she says.

The security guards, seeing that their inpregnable shield of defense has already been breached by a short blond girlie, wave Tim and Tanya through their ranks with a collective shaking of heads and tutting of tongues.

Tim and Tanya stop dead, looking at me with a kind of glowing admiration that borders on the scary. "Oh . . . wow," says Tanya, a mass of suppressed hand gestures. Tim seems to be lost for words. I get the distinct impression that he's trying not to shed a tear of joy. Unable to contain herself any longer, Tanya hurls herself around Tim and envelops him in swirls of arms and hair. All I can see of him is his boggling eyes.

Reporters are massing around the security guards, firing questions at me that I suddenly find I can't even listen to anymore. Too much. A makeshift press conference is being convened at the signing table.

The crowd is calmer now, more ordered, as the guards and the T-shirted shop staff contain things with raised voices and outstretched arms. TV cameras get slung onto operators' shoulders, lights blink, journalists make phone calls, a couple of TV newshounds record quick pieces to camera. Flanked by guards, Emma, Tim, Tanya and I walk around the CD displays to stand with a clear view of Lisa, sitting at the table, watching the storm abate around her. We're between "Classical" and "Easy Listening A–Z," beneath a giant square of cardboard hanging in midair proclaiming the urgency of a visit to the second-floor coffee shop.

"Hi, everyone. I have something to say," says Lisa into the wide bank of microphones in front of her.

Click flash click.

"I'd just like to say thanks for your, err, concern, but I'm fine, and so is—"

"How do you feel, Lisa?"

"Are you in need of medical treatment, Lisa?"

"Are you going to sue Big Deal Records, Lisa?"

She pauses for a second. "I've been parked on my backside for a couple of hours. It's not a national emergency. Let's stay in the real world, shall we? What I want to say is . . ."

She looks over to me. Our eyes meet, and now I can read a lot in the vague smile that twitches at the corners of her mouth. I smile back.

". . . simply that, as of today, I'll be canceling all my scheduled signings and other appointments for the foreseeable future. Obviously, I don't want to disappoint Plastic fans, and—"

Everything else she says is swamped in noise and movement.

"Lisa!"

"Are you leaving the band, Lisa? Are you leaving the band?"

"Has being helplessly trapped in a lift made you decide this, Lisa?"

"Are you on the edge of a nervous breakdown, Lisa?"

"Lisa!"

"Lisa, are you leaving the band?"

Tanya whirls on her heels and gapes at me. "OhmyGodoh myGodohmyGod! What the hell happened to her in there? What did she say to you? What did you say to her?"

I shrug. "Nothing much."

Tanya and Tim start to push their way into the crowd, to get closer to her. Emma is holding on to my arm, as if she's the only thing stopping me from being swallowed up in a tornado of news coverage. With a sudden burst of concentrated resolve, I turn to her and look her square in the face.

"Don't go out with Tim," I say. "Please. Go out with me."

She blinks a couple of times. "He's not, like, my BOYFRIEND or anything. We've only been to the cinema."

"Whatever he's said I've said, I didn't mean, really, truly. I'm so, SO sorry. You mean the world to me, I promise."

Her head shifts back on that smooth, elegant neck of hers. She blinks some more. "He's not said anything to . . . Sorry, what are you saying?"

"I'm saying I'm the biggest berk of all time." I notice the CDs to one side of me. I slip one that seems familiar out of the rack. "Bach. Is this one any good?"

Emma's entire body radiates the kind of frozen disbelief you normally only see in comedy movies when someone walks in on something. "I've . . . got a copy at home."

"Maybe we could listen to it sometime?"

She looks up at me. Those eyes, warming every atom of me.

"You are . . . Dominic Smith . . . aren't you? You're not some bloke with a rubber mask and a strange sense of humor?"

"No," I say confidently. "I'm the real Dominic Smith."

The noise of the crowd is on the rise again. Fans are milling about as if milling about were the perfect substitute for thought. Reporters are jostling angrily amongst themselves. Lisa is standing beside the table, bathed in the flashing lights and the unending questions, letting it all wash off her. Tim and Tanya are steadily wading through people, heading through stormy waters to the safety of Lisa's side. The shop manager and Bob Fullbright are nowhere to be seen.

Emma places a hand on my chest. "Hang on a minute. What's this you've said to Tim about me, then?"

"Nothing," I say quickly.

"You and I belong together
Kicking girl, inspired fella
One hundred percent of lurve"

—"100% Love," from the compilation album *Plastic: Greatest Hits*
(Voyd/Parkins © Cellophane Music Ltd)

So. There you have it. The story of how I met Lisa Voyd and ended up destroying the hopes and dreams of Plastic fans the world over.

I have a feeling Tim and Tanya may never forgive me. After the Incident in the Lift they started badgering me relentlessly about what was said to whom by whom and when. And I told them that whatever was said was a private conversation, thanks very much, and they went off in a huff. Via Tim's Web site, I got e-mails from fans all over the world once the news broke internationally. I sent out a standard "no comment" reply.

Lisa Trapped in Lift

Voyd Ditches Plastic: Music World Stunned

Lift Horror Turns Lisa's Mind

The tidal wave of sewage took a few days to drain away. I had newspapers ringing me, or turning up at home, which drove Mum potty. When Mum was out, Gran kept supplying the reporters on the doorstep with cups of tea and the complete history of Grandad's bowels. The reporters stopped coming after a while.

Tim and Tanya, meanwhile, are very much an item these days. I think what's thrown them together is the intensity of the pop music tragedy which they so intimately witnessed and survived. That, and their mutual suspicions about what was said to whom by whom and when. Suspicions intensified, of course, once the breakup of Plastic got announced a few weeks later. They're both in the same boat now that the saga of Plastic has come to an end. Tim's Web site is still a shrine to the band and its music, but there's an air of mourning about it now, and I think they're both a bit unsure of what to do with their free time.

Lisa's devoted herself to songwriting. I hear she's writing for a couple of new bands—one's called the Effects and the other's called Fat, believe it or not. If you haven't heard of them yet, then you soon will. You'll be humming those songs along with the rest of us.

As for the other members of Plastic, they weren't exactly pleased to find the rug pulled from under their feet. All three of them said some pretty nasty things about Lisa in interviews. Mike Parkins and Sean Appleby formed a management company. Kurt Bartrom joined a Dutch band who are huge in the Middle East, apparently.

And what, I hear you cry, of our dashing hero?

It feels strange, now that Plastic are part of the past. Part of everyone's past. But there's something oddly comforting about the way they've taken their place in pop history. They have a beginning, a middle and an end.

Their story is complete. Mine, on the other hand, definitely isn't.

Be a writer, said Emma, remember? So I thought I'd give it a go. See how it fits. This is the result.

And Emma? Well, we've always had a laugh together, haven't we? I'm still not sure I'll ever actually understand her, but at least it's a mind-expanding experience trying.

In a few weeks, it'll be Christmas again.

ABOUT THE AUTHOR

Simon Cheshire is the author of several popular books for young readers published in the United Kingdom. His first book for Delacorte Press, *Kissing Vanessa,* was praised as "flat-out uproarious" *(Kirkus Reviews)* and "earnest [and] openhearted" (*The Bulletin,* Recommended). He also writes and presents "Fast Foreword," a bluffer's guide to literature, on Oneword Radio and is constantly fiddling about with his Web site at http://uk.geocities.com/simoncheshireuk. He writes in a tiny little office that used to be a closet, where he'd be helpless without his Mac and a regular supply of chocolate. Most of his best ideas come to him while he's asleep or staring out the window. He lives in Warwick, England, but spends most of his time in the world of the strange and unusual.